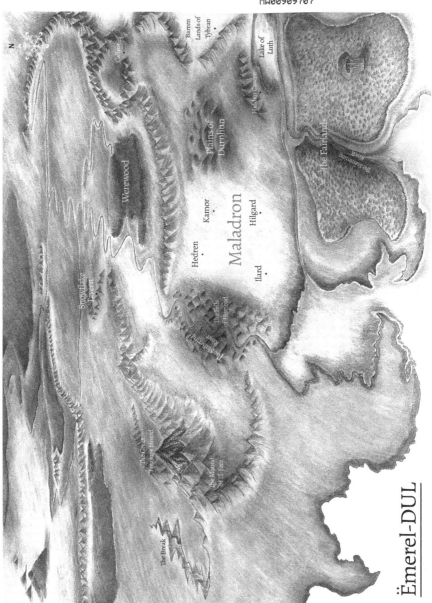

Barren
Lands of
Tyban

Culin

Lake of
Luth

Plains of
Durnhtun

Werewood

Maladron

Hedren

Kamor

Hilgard

Ilard

The Fairlands

Snowflake
Tavern

The Fells
of Fleimred

The Great
Dragons Hoard

The Mound
of Ill-Fate

The Break

Ëmerel-DUL

WELTHERON
THE WINTER DESTINY

J. J. P. TALONSKEI

LifeRich PUBLISHING

LifeRich Publishing is a registered trademark of The Reader's Digest Association, Inc.

LifeRich Publishing books may be ordered through booksellers or by contacting:

LifeRich Publishing
1663 Liberty Drive
Bloomington, IN 47403
www.liferichpublishing.com
1 (888) 238-8637

Cover & Chapter 12 Illustrations by Zan Vickers
Map & Chapters 1 - 11 Illustrations by J. J. P. Talonskei

ISBN: 978-1-4897-2490-8 (sc)
ISBN: 978-1-4897-2491-5 (hc)
ISBN: 978-1-4897-2492-2 (e)

Library of Congress Control Number: 2019914479

Print information available on the last page.

LifeRich Publishing rev. date: 9/18/2019

I'm dedicating this book to my brother, John,
who will do great things someday and
is going to change the world.

AUTHOR'S NOTE

Like most kids, there was a time when I felt pain and fear of my peers looking down on me. This crippled my confidence as I grew older, and self-doubt became a familiar companion. One of the ways I dealt with this was through my imagination. As a kid, my mind was always active. Tales of villains and protagonists took me on adventures as they fought with swords, sailed the high seas, and narrowly escaped dire circumstances. All these adventurous tales continually played out in my head as I grew older.

I managed to escape being phyiscally bullied while growing up (mainly because I was homeschooled, and I had four other brothers to protect me), but I did suffer from verbal bullying and had my share of false accusations and rejection. All these things forced me to retreat into a world that existed in my own head, a world that was safe … one I could control.

I started writing when I was fourteen. It was a way I dealt with the negative emotions in my head. I'd try to channel that energy to help create something positive and inspiring. From a young age, I always had a love for writing fantasy fiction. It had become an emerging passion, a general belief that, like a book, I couldn't just put it back on the shelf and never open it again.

As I neared the end of my high school years, I felt that the passion and inspiration to write had started to wane. Suddenly I didn't have the drive anymore. It became hard for me to create characters and come up with an idea that was outside the box, something that took people on an entirely different adventure. Other personal problems also surfaced as I contemplated what next steps to take in life. I was never really interested in going to college and felt like most of the world around me uttered that same lie that said that if a person didn't go to college, he or she wasn't considered smart. This belief really discouraged me as a young adult. A fresh batch of false accusations surfaced from people I thought were my friends. I was not only pushed away, but I also felt scared inside for no reasonable cause. It felt as if I were being scorched by my "fire-breathing" friends with negative words.

At twenty-three years of age, I felt like I had hit rock bottom. The fear of not being accepted and the false accusations had sucked the life right out of me. After being betrayed by people I had once considered my friends, it was hard for me to be social again. But not just social. I had trouble being friendly and open. Because of this tendency, I felt ugly, almost like a monster (despite the fact that inside, I was as timid as a lamb). The fairy tales in my head suddenly became real again. Only this time, I was the protagonist, and those who had wronged me in life were the villains, dragons if you will; and the hurt and rejection were really the fire that burned. I needed a way to confront these "dragons" and their fire. I would breathe not fire but frost that turned to ice. Even though I was an outcast, I used this idea to protect myself and those I cared about. I could do all sorts of things with it. I realized it was my shield against the flames. I found I could save others from the pain of fire. I could defeat the fire of hatred and wrath with the cooling blanket of frost.

In this story, the main character, *Weltheron*, this tale's hero, becomes painfully aware of how different he is when compared to the rest of his kind. He struggles to find his place. It is only through many heroic adventures that he is brought face-to-face with his differences ... and with himself. And through the acceptance of his differences, he discovers the greatness and power of his diversity. In time, what he at first thinks is weakness suddenly becomes strength. The weakness of his caring and mercy forces him not only from his home but also from his family. What he comes to realize is that his powers are the only things that can save his world from utter destruction and that he mustn't fear them. Only his enemies should.

—J. J. P. Talonskei

CONTENTS

Prologue xiii

1 A Secret Meeting 1
2 An Unpleasant Encounter 9
3 The Winter Destiny .19
4 A Cold Welcome 31
5 The Treason of Ganther 43
6 Making Amends 51
7 The Fairlands 59
8 The Battle of Maladron 65
9 Warning Signs 73
10 A Bargaining 81
11 Know Your Destiny .93
12 The Renaissance of Destiny 101

Acknowledgments 109

PROLOGUE

In the world of Ëmerel-DUL, there was a mysterious and secret order of magicians, known as the Ëmerels. As history tells us, they were the keepers and bringers of peace and prosperity in the land (among other things). They possessed many secret powers. The most dangerous of these was Altering Destinies, otherwise known as the Unbreakable Spell.

When a destiny was changed, it was no small event. The land, animals, and entire kingdom seemed to reflect a certain confusion, disorder, or bewilderment, if you will. To the Ancient One, the Ëmerels' creator, Semper, this power was especially forbidden; and they alone heard his voice. It was Semper who brought harmony to the three Ëmerels, and it was his power that was equal to that of the three. Semper named his creation Ëmerel-DUL. The last three letters of Ëmerel-DUL he intended to indicate three words, which defined him: Deity, Unity, and Lasting.

Ages after the awakening of beings in Ëmerel-DUL, the three keepers stopped hearing Semper's voice. Something disturbing had come to settle in the land. A newly hatched evil had found its way, and confusion now reigned. And so begins the tale of Weltheron.

1

A SECRET MEETING

SNOWFLAKE TAVERN WAS a place found up in the Freezing Mountains, near Stone-Cold Pass. It wasn't a place many common folk visited often, mainly because … well, it was stone cold. Only the dwarf miners visited with any frequency—that is, those who had mines—and those were deep in the mountains. They would trade gold and silver for pints of ale and warm, cozy beds at night.

The inn was hewn into the side of the mountain. Its exposed exterior was a hand-sawn beech with a limestone footing. Snowflake, as others called it, rose three stories high, clutching the side of the mountain. Above the entrance, a sign, frozen over with snow, bore the mark of the snowflake. The front door was the same wood with hammered iron hinges and a handle with a neat, round window perched at the top. Just inside was a large room with wooden walls and ancient beams angling up to the ceiling. To the right was a bar to purchase drink, food, or a room for the night. To the left was a stone fireplace with a great roaring fire. Many were huddled around it, warming their hands.

There were all sorts of voices throughout the room. All the customers, dwarves, sang the famous song that was often sung in Snowflake Tavern. It went like this.

The place to stay, where the ale's an upgrade,
Is up in Snowflake Tavern.

For days and days, we've toiled away
Till we're all but spent and famished.

If it weren't for Jack, we'd be in shaft
In every hall and cavern, but instead we're snug
With a cupful mug up in Snowflake Tavern.

What keeps the brutal cold at bay? It's hard to say.
It's as if it were predestined.

It matters not; we're served with draught
And every comfort of home.

So if you're lost, it's worth the cost to stay
Up at Snowflake Tavern.

The dwarves of those mountains had a certain knack for inventing themes and sang them merrily throughout the evening. Amid the dwarves sat an old man, hooded and cloaked in black. He had a long, grey beard, and he sat at a table by himself near a window covered in sleet.

It was half past midnight, and the old man had ridden there. Rather, he had flown there on a somewhat strange beast. He had come a long way and had wanted to bring his steed inside; but the innkeeper, clad in a leathery, worn gown and apron, objected to this, saying, "All livestock are not allowed in here. Anyone knows that!"

The old man replied, "He's not livestock and is a friend. It's a good thing for you that he didn't insist on coming in here. He told me his furry wings would keep him warm and that your stable should be sufficient."

"Who do you think you are, old man?" retorted the innkeeper. "I have a good mind to kick you out—or even better, call my landlord and have him do it."

"Call your landlord; I have business with him anyway," said the old man.

At this the innkeeper was surprised. He knew what his master was capable of and how he dealt with upset customers.

"It's your funeral, old man," remarked the innkeeper, and he went off to find his landlord. Upon returning with his master, he sought to spin a tale—a different version of the truth—but suddenly, he became mute. The master was brought to dismay.

The landlord's complexion was somewhat young looking but not quite since he was in truth ages old. He was average in stature and had short, scraggly, blondish hair along with a unique mustache and a goatee under his chin. His eyes were light blue. He wasn't clad in majestic garments, but then again, they weren't shabby. His clothes were dark blue, and he wore an apron over them. His garments were trimmed with white fur, which made them a bit more expensive than usual, and on his feet he wore leather boots like everyone else.

Once face-to-face with the stranger, the landlord pitched his apron, and when he did, the old man saw that he wore a white belt around his waist with a golden buckle and a vibrant amulet like his own. But this one was of a silver-plated snowflake. The old man, rising to his feet, spoke in an intriguing manner. "Jack Winter, is it not? The one in our order otherwise called Frost Master?"

The landlord, who looked puzzled, replied in a similar manner but with added wit. "You have me at somewhat of a disadvantage, old friend, but I think I know your name. Wait, don't tell me; you are the one called Weather Shaper, are you not? But is it the Enchanter Casmin?"

"You have guessed right. Yes, Casmin is my name. You're a hard man to find, and you're still as keen as I once remember you, Jack Winter," replied Casmin. "I see you have kept your youthfulness as well."

With that, the innkeeper's muteness left him, and he was baffled as to why he couldn't speak. But that didn't stop him from asking his landlord, "You know this old miser?"

"This old miser still has tricks up his sleeve," retorted the Enchanter.

"Everything is fine, Thad," Jack said to the innkeeper. "I'll take things from here. Casmin and I will return to my lodgings. Make sure we aren't disturbed," he added. And with that, they were immediately caught up in conversation. Jack asked Casmin how he'd found him, and the Enchanter told him that he'd talked to friends who had friends in the mountains, and that was how he had figured out Jack's location.

They passed through a corridor until they came to another main door. Jack threw the door open, and both of them walked in. It was Jack's hall, for his inn was only a concealment of that. In truth, he was one of the three Ëmerels, and so was Casmin.

The Ëmerels were a secret order and had to be, for they didn't seek to alter destinies by their presence, only to bring about peace and prosperity. It was the law of their order to be greatly concerned with matters that involved threats to their world, but they worked without anyone knowing. Jack was proud of his hall, which was quite spacious, with ice columns running up and down each side of the main room. The ground reflected everything, as if a mirror, and between each column were shelves of books Jack loved reading. He was particularly fond of the study of insects since he was fascinated with how little yet intriguing these creatures were. He never saw them in person since he was accustomed to the bitter cold, not to the warmer climates below the mountains.

What Jack loved most, though, about his hall was his glazed snowball—a "magic frost-seer," it was called. This was placed on a wooden table in the center of the room. He used the thing as a means of spying from a distance. It also gave him the ability of foresight into the future and hindsight into the past.

Of course, every Ëmerel, including Casmin, could see to and fro in time, but one thing that was dangerous about this ability was that it temped them to alter their own and others' destinies, which was exactly what the keepers were not to do. Now, sometimes destines were meant to be altered but rarely—and if they were, this was meant to happen gradually and not with a forcible hand. This was what Casmin discovered Jack had done, and it didn't go unnoticed by the Ëmerel.

"What have you done, Frost?" asked Casmin. For short, he called the Frost Master by this name. "You were only supposed to keep an eye on those creatures and their offspring. Instead, you broke the gravest of rules of our order and altered the destiny of a creature that we do not even fully understand yet! How and why did you carry out such a risky task, if I may ask?"

"My actions may have seemed hasty," replied Jack. "But reaching into that hive and infusing my magic mark into that egg seemed like a brilliant idea at the time. Don't worry; I placed it back in the nest without anyone noticing."

"We're dealing with a race of creatures so powerful and unpredictable that it is unlikely they would ever come to change their ways. You're playing with fire, Frost, and that is not safe, particularly for you."

"Maybe I am, Enchanter, but just maybe this act could change the course of things for the better. What I saw in future things was the renaissance of destiny—a rebirth, if you will. Don't you remember the ancient truths found in legend? There is one that describes my point best. Here, I will read it to you," said the Frost Master, grasping an old book from the shelves nearby. From it, he read, "'For every age, there will rise an offspring, one in a million … like unto one star amid many … that one will stay the hand of evil to correct the path of weakened beings.'"

After reciting this, Jack shut the book. "This creature has no idea what it's capable of yet, and when it grows up, it will be a force not to be trifled with. That is, with the help of a few added touches of my magic."

"What added touches do you mean, Frost Master?" asked the Enchanter.

At this, a sly look came over Jack's face. In response, he only stared back at the Enchanter as if telling him what it was.

The Enchanter at once guessed what Jack was hinting and turned in disappointment. Lifting his hood from his head, letting his long strands of grey hair fall, he breathed deeply. This wasn't the only matter that troubled him, for farther down below the mountains, there was talk of war where the realms of men and other beings dwelt.

This was the last thing that needed to happen, especially with such a great force out there building up. This was what Casmin and Jack were discussing. It was only a matter of time before things would get worse and the fate of races would face utter annihilation. On top of things, there was something else wrong that troubled Casmin.

The Enchanter, coming to a concluding thought, turned and faced Jack. "There is more than just altering destinies at stake here, Frost Master. Tempers are flaring below the mountains, and to make matters worse, one of the three Ëmerels has gone missing. I'm sure you remember him, Jack. The one called Shadow Walker, Ganther the Concealer. When I came to call on him the same as you, his dwelling concealed beneath a mountain slope in the east was abandoned. I fear something terrible has gone ill. I tried searching the past to find out what had befallen him, but because his magic conceals, all I could see was black and nothing more. Without Ganther, a great deal of questions are left unanswered. He is the only other piece we need of the three in order to figure out if your scheme, Jack, is a hindrance or a solution to the future. You may have seen promising things, but what really matters is the outcome. And that is farther than what our gift of foresight can show us."

2

AN UNPLEASANT ENCOUNTER

A DARK AND MENACING-LOOKING mountain had arisen eighteen thousand feet in the west, towering over a terrain of mountain peaks that surrounded it. This smaller line of mountains, veering farther south, were called the "Claw" because they curled in sort of a hook and were regarded as such by all who dwelled in Ëmerel-DUL. The reason for such a massive rise of rock was a giant meteor that had fallen out of the sky long ago. It had been larger than any other heft of stone that entered that atmosphere. Its outer crust was a glassy black, similar to that of obsidian stone. It was at one time part of a planet—a dying planet, in fact. And now it was a hive (a Great Treasure Hoard) and home to dragons. Yes, dragons dwelt within this mass of rock, in which caverns had been hewn all across the outer face of its climb. Stone as rare as this mysteriously held rich deposits of gold. It also contained gems and other valuable jewels, which made it a remarkable score and find for dragons, and it was worth more than several kings' ransoms.

A mountain this vast could shelter hundreds of fire-breathers at a time. Each dragon had its own hold or claim, and it didn't have to go on raids because it was already filthy rich. Every one of these beasts was neither monstrous nor small in size. They were neither foul nor evil- looking dragons, and they were horselike in aspect and feature, with webbed ears that looked like wings.

Every year these pillagers of the sky had their offspring (and not just a few) and dozens of eggs until their holds were overflowing. It was August 15 of the fourth age, and there was a particular family of dragons, called Sëiron the Brown and Garthayn the Grey. This was going to be their forty-seventh time to have dragonlings. Over the years, Garthayn had borne over a thousand young. Most were full grown by now and dwelt in other hives far abroad. Some of them had since become excellent Raiders and made some impressive hauls back to their hoards. They were moving up in the ranks as far as being looked up to and respected by their fellow Raiders. For many years, though, the dragons of this great hive didn't go on raids, and what is more, they didn't need to. They kept a watchful eye on their existing spoils, waiting for the day when their tribe grew larger and had to start new hives somewhere else in Ëmerel-DUL.

Sëiron and Garthayn had seventy-three eggs in their hold. They all began to hatch gradually until they came down to one last egg. Like the rest, this egg's shell had a smooth and glassy exterior look. Only it was white and tossed and turned until finely hatched. From the shell emerged a small dragonling that was as white as snow. The parents were confused when they saw it. Dragon eggs were typically red, brown, orange, purple, green, blue, and any other color for that matter but never usually white.

Garthayn, the mother dragon, went over to inspect their newborn. It was no doubt a male dragonling, and it was branded on its forehead with what at first appeared to be a birthmark. But it was, in fact, an odd-shaped rune; and surrounding this symbol were a series of dots that mysteriously formed a circle around it. They seemed to form the outline of a star and had webbed points.

The dragonling sneezed, but it didn't spurt flame; rather, out came a cloud of frost that turned to ice when it hit the ground. The parents, upon witnessing this, were brought to dismay. They didn't know what to think of their newborn. The father dragon, Sëiron, was distressed.

"Should we tell someone?" he asked. "This has never happened before, and the clan might protest to a white, frost-breathing dragon."

"They will find out soon enough," remarked Garthayn. "It should not make any difference. He's one of us and is special. I would never cast aside or maroon one of our own just because they are different." And with that Garthayn, taking hold of her newborn, said to Sëiron, "I will call him Weltheron, for that is a fitting name for him, and he wears it well."

Sëiron agreed, and both parents cuddled with their newborn.

It didn't take long for all the parents' little dragonlings to start to grow up. Several months passed, and nearly all of them were half fully grown, including Weltheron. His scalelike armor was now a silver-white hue, and the irises of this male dragon's eyes were deep blue, like sapphires. One might say Weltheron was extremely passive and practically tame by nature. He was somewhat playful and didn't in the least desire to be a Raider, plundering riches and storing up great wealth for himself.

This was only part of what he felt inside. When he realized he was different and not like other dragons, he saw this contrast as a weakness. Often he heard the rest of his brothers and sisters, who were fire-breathers, talk about how someday they would become excellent Raiders and rule hives of their own. All this conversation made him feel like he didn't fit in with his kind, and as the days followed, he became less intrigued with the thought of one day becoming a Raider himself.

Near the end of spring, all young firedrakes were sent to trials. This entailed each dragon youngster being judged on how to master its instinctive abilities by other adult dragons, who were teachers. Weltheron didn't want to go to trials and wished he could stay home, but his parents insisted. He also had no choice in the matter, since all offspring were under the law and required to attend trials.

The day dawned when Weltheron and all his siblings, along with his father, Sëiron, departed from their hive. Their destination was the Break, a deep crack in the earth, made long ago from loose debris of a giant meteor, which had come from the one the dragons lived in. Such a deep impression was now a valley, which measured seven thousand feet high and extended fifteen miles west of the map. It was mainly a vast dried-up gorge, save for plants, such as cactuses, which grew in numerous quantity there. But where most of the life grew was farther below the great ravine, at the bottom, where a river also flowed. It was called the Break due to the fact that all young firedrakes were sent there to be broken in; and by this, they were trained to become Raiders.

Weltheron's mother, Garthayn, stayed behind to watch over their house of spoils. It was customary for the adult females to guard the holds while the adult males were away. The family of dragons looked like a swarm of birds from above, only they weren't birds but living terrors that ruled the skies in that world and flew at greater heights and altitudes than any other bird of prey. Weltheron and his father, flying side by side, conversed most of the way to the Break.

"What is it that our kind fears the most, if not any other creature?" asked Weltheron.

"What we fear the most is our leader. You'd best stand clear of him, Son, if you don't want trouble. If you cross him, that is all you will get, trouble, and he will hurt you greatly. Your wounds will be deep if you challenge his authority in the clan. The 'Black Terror,' they call him, but his real name is Glaider, Lord Glaider the Black, and you should fear him. His wrath is like no other fire-breather I've ever seen. His size is greater than any foregoing lord I have served. His fire none can equal, and his patience is short."

Weltheron wanted to know more and asked, "How did he become lord over us, and how long has he been lord?"

"Long enough as I know it," remarked Sëiron. "He became lord less than an age ago and won't be handing that title over anytime soon. I still remember the last lord that held honor in the clan. He was called Thrarg the Green. A wise Raider, he was, but not bloodthirsty like Glaider. He's the one who brought our kind to these lands of Ëmerel-DUL and discovered the Great Treasure Hoard that is now our home. After all this, Glaider showed up, and I watched him pick apart the old lord limb by limb until there was nothing left. Where the likes of this nomad came from, no one knows, my son. All I know is, you should never cross him, or else you will regret it."

Weltheron, pondering all this, was brought to distress. His father didn't want to frighten him but wanted him to know what kind of terror Glaider was and the consequences involved if he were to accidently cross such a monster. During the rest of the way, Weltheron didn't say another word, and with each beat of his wings, he became more nervous the closer they came to the Break.

Upon reaching the valley, the family of dragons gradually descended. Once they passed over the dropping point, there suddenly appeared a sight Weltheron would never forget. And that was the sight of hundreds of dragons all gathered atop a vast continental slope, which hung over a lower one like a shelf. There were so many of them that Weltheron couldn't count them. He lost count after ninety-seven. He and his family, seventy-four of them there were, including his father, landed in one specific area of the valley that wasn't as crowded.

There were many young dragons, males and females and juveniles, who stood amid where they had landed, all seeming to be caught up in conversation. Weltheron's father left them there and joined a group of adults, who stood nearby. Weltheron and his siblings were unsure of what to do. One of his sisters, a female called Lyeera the Blue, whispered in Weltheron's ear and asked him, "What should we do? I already have enough brothers and sisters as it is. I don't want to get to know anyone else besides them."

"Come on, Lyeera," replied Weltheron. "There's more to you

than that. I'm willing to give it a try if you will. Pretty soon I don't think we'll have much choice in the matter anyways, seeing as how these are trials and we are students and will have teachers. We had better just get it over with."

Just then there arose a loud bellow from an adult, who stood aloft a high perch in the ravine. His voice echoed throughout the entire chasm, reaching the ears of every single dragon gathered there.

"All right, it's time to begin," roared the adult. "All young firedrakes will fall in line, and each will take his or her turn for every trial. There will be three trials, and each one you will complete, or Lord Glaider will have a bone to pick with you. Now, buck up and get a move on!"

"Come on," said Weltheron to Lyeera. "Follow me, and we can get in line."

When at last most dragons had completed their trial, it was Weltheron's turn. This trial involved speed. The dragons' job was to catch falcons nesting nearby in the canyon and were judged based on how many they caught in a certain amount of time. This test took skill, and some students had difficulty catching *any* of these swift birds. Weltheron managed to catch two falcons and got lucky; he snatched up two at the same time as they crossed in front of him in flight. After the trial was over, Weltheron ate these scores as snacks. To him, falcon tasted all right, but his favorite was mountain goat, which he and family hunted often.

The second trial involved being invisible. It was more a hide-and-seek trial than anything else. This also Weltheron did very well in—for being a white dragon, that is. Blending in with one's surroundings was something all fire-breathers had to be good at. As for Weltheron, since he wasn't like other dragons, he could surprisingly blend in well with water, something dragons wouldn't go near when trying to camouflage themselves. There was just something about dragons and water that didn't go well together ... that, is until now.

From above Weltheron had spied the river that flowed beneath the gorge as he and family had flown there. One thing the frost-breather's parents had taught him about water supply was that if the water didn't come from the surface, it most likely was spring fed. Spring water was not only fresh but also usually frigid, because it flowed under the ground and was kept cool. This spring water was something the frost-breather blended in with best, and his scales, acting the same as pigments, could easily absorb wavelengths of light and color. Then he could project them again, making himself invisible to the naked eye. Of course, every dragon needed to remain completely still for this effect to happen.

Once landing amid the lower parts of the valley, Weltheron waded into the stream. It was definitely icy cold, a perfect temperature his changing coat of scales adapted well to. The dragon, bending as low as he could beneath the surface of the water, made himself appear as a boulder lying amid the water. This choice worked better than any of the other dragons' hiding places. The adults not only had a difficult time finding him but also took them longer than usual. After he succeeded in being the last one found in this trial, Weltheron was proud of himself, knowing he had proved he was one of the clan, even if he was different. Sëiron was also proud of his son and wished him to prove that, despite his lack of breathing fire, he could still be a Raider.

It came time for the last and final trial, the most important of the three; and that was for a dragon to prove he or she was a merciless Raider. The law of the tribe said that "any dragon should kill at all cost in order to gain great wealth." It was the cruel rule of the clan, and every Raider had to obey it. This trial required killing dwarves, and because these people were known to dwell so high in the mountains, they were easy victims for the dragons to capture and use for sport such as this. Before the trial began, the dwarves were kept in deep craters, which were like holes below the ravine. Eventually the adults flew down, and upon freeing the dwarves from their holes, they gave all the captives a chance to escape. Each young dragon's task was to see how many Dwarves they could catch and devour. To Weltheron this seemed like a very unpleasant task. He became nervous when the command was given for him and the rest of the students to attack.

Taking flight, the white dragon was off to a bad start. He purposely dodged three victims and tried his best to cover up his mistakes, but eyes were watching everywhere, including a certain pair of eyes belonging to a black adult, who rested beneath an overhang of rock that overlooked the entire valley below. Weltheron's father watched in distress from a distance, hoping nothing would go wrong. The frost-breather felt his heart pounding and, knowing his place, saw a moving target. He took a dive, surging downward at a great speed.

His victim, while in his flight to get away, turned and saw the dragon upon him. At that instant, he was met with a sudden impact, which sent him falling backward and on his back. Thinking he was done for, the dwarf shut his eyes and waited for a swift death. But for a long while, nothing happened. The dwarf, slowly opening his eyes and seeing the dragon standing over him, noticed that the beast's eyes were shut and its head bent. The pale dragon, peering down at the dwarf, bore a look of pity in his eyes.

With no restraint, Weltheron released his talons from the dwarf's chest. The dwarf, realizing the dragon wouldn't harm him, quickly rose. At first, he was in awe; then, gazing about, he spied a small cave in the rock nearby. Immediately, he ran toward it as fast as he could to escape. Amidst of his flight, a shadow fell upon him.

It turned out to be the black firedrake watching from above. With one fell swoop, it snatched the dwarf up, devouring him forthrightly, and landed on the ground. It was Glaider himself. With fury in his eyes, he changed course and advanced back toward the small dragon. Like a dark cloud, Glaider hovered over Weltheron. The adult's eyes burned like fiery coals, and from his nostrils, he exhaled rays like blue flame. His black hide of scales, as dark as night, was bristly and grainy, mainly because of rock sediment that had formed on it over the years. The sediment buildup meant this beast rarely stirred from its hold, and the constant changing of weather in the mountains accounted for it. From this alpha dragon's head grew a pair of long horns, and under his chin sprouted stubs that were like tusks. All these extra things told you he was more than just a dragon. He looked as if he were a ridiculously monstrous bat, and unlike other dragons, he crawled about with arms and wings attached. Glaider fell on Weltheron with harsh words, and the young dragon became frightened and bent low to the ground.

"Do you defy the law of the clan?" Glaider bellowed in a loud and demanding voice.

In a low-pitched voice, Weltheron replied, "I don't, but I am afraid to kill an innocent creature."

"Innocent creature? They are our enemies and, once more, prey," remarked the dragon lord. "You are a weakling if you think such a creature is innocent. Your scale is white, young firedrake, which to me breathes unusual. Ah, you must be that loner, the frost-breather that has a distaste for fire, aren't you? You remind me of someone I once knew. He was like you but not quite. But it matters not. I will destroy them, along with everyone else, and fulfill the destiny I have chosen. You bring dishonor to this clan."

Just as Glaider was about to assail him with more words, Weltheron's father, Sëiron, suddenly appeared between the large dragon and his son.

"My son means to admit that he had eaten his fill of prey and can eat no more. He means no disrespect to you, my liege," he further added.

At hearing this, the stern dragon relented but said next time there would be consequences if this happened again. With a grunt, he departed and returned to his high place of honor.

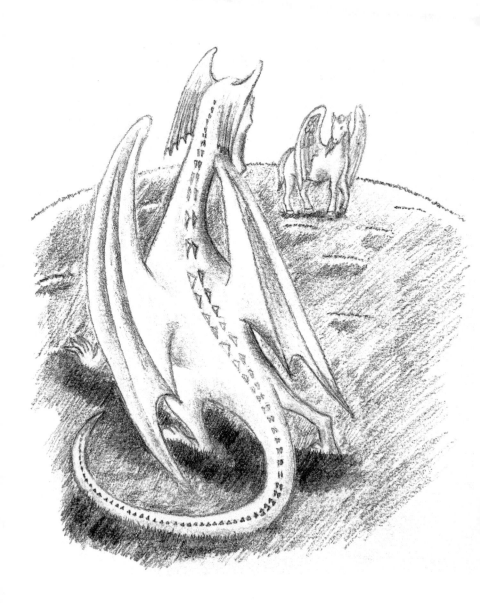

3

THE WINTER DESTINY

B ACK AT THE hold, there was much discussion about Weltheron's unpleasant encounter with Glaider. Weltheron's parents were upset with him but worried at the same time. Glaider's warning wasn't to be taken lightly, and if things didn't change, there could be one less dragon in the clan.

"Don't you know you could have been killed?" remarked Weltheron's father. "It was a good thing for you that I was there to save you, or else he would have. And don't forget his remark about you being a frost-breather. One less dragon that isn't a fire-breather makes no difference to Glaider."

"Enough, Sëiron," interrupted Garthayn. "My son, there are some things you must realize. Glaider is a fierce dragon and set in his ways. There is no telling what he will do. But whatever happens, you must obey, even when you do not understand. When we had you, Weltheron, you were different from the rest, but we have treated you no differently than any of your brothers or sisters."

The parents' white dragon was drenched in tears. There was just something inside him that couldn't bring him to want to kill. Everything about Weltheron was different, from his scale being the hue of white to being a frost-breather and now going against the law of the clan. The only thing that was the same was that he was a dragon, but even that name didn't suit him. Something just didn't add up.

"There is only one thing you must understand," added Weltheron's father in a somewhat stern voice, "and that is that you can't change what you are."

Weltheron was silent for a moment, then replied, "I may never come to understand the ways of our kind since I am different. You said so yourselves. I have no place in this hive."

After he said this, he went deeper into his hole. His parents didn't press on him more words, having already warned him of the danger involved.

That night at the Great Treasure Hoard, Weltheron couldn't sleep. Several times, he stirred and walked over to the entrance of his hole, which was half covered in spoil and riches. These were scattered about on the floor, which his parents had given him as an allowance. But as the days followed, Weltheron grew only less and less concerned about great wealth and desired none of it.

"What a disgrace I have turned out to be," he said to himself. "There must be a reason for all this. I won't kill for the sake of it or be bullied by an oversized bat. I am different, and I need to know why."

He thought intently about the whole matter and of what his parents had told him before. *What must I do?* he wondered. The only thing left was to run away and seek answers. He hated the thought of leaving his parents, but he had no choice.

As silently as he could, he crept out of his hole, trying not to tap his claws against the stone floor for fear that the sound might wake the others. There was a main corridor that ran outside his nest, which in turn led to the main entrance of the cave. The interior of the cavern was quite large, extending far into the mountain, and had to be for a family as big as Weltheron's. On either side of the corridor, there were countless hollows lining the walls. A few hundred of them there were, all belonging to Weltheron's brothers and sisters. The last hollow Weltheron passed was that of his parents. Whispering, he said farewell to them and to his home, which he doubted he would ever see again. Then he took flight, flying aimlessly toward the north.

As he flew, he looked back with great regret but knew he couldn't stay. As he turned one last time, he saw the Great Treasure Hoard and all the caves running up and down. Suddenly they grew faint in the distance and vanished behind the towering mountain peaks. He flew through half the night over mountain terrain, valleys, and kingdoms until he was sure he was far enough from the Great Treasure Hoard. Along the way, he came across a patch of green on a hillside. It looked uninhabited from above, for dragons have keen eyesight, especially at night. Swiftly and steadily, he landed on this small patch of green. He saw all around that there were rabbit holes and thick brush, which made it a perfect place to sleep.

"Splendid," said Weltheron to himself, furling his wings and making a place with his reptile paws. Afterward, he collapsed wearily on the soft earth, which was cushion like and drifted off.

The sky was a royal blue, and the stars had vanished the next morning, save for the moon, which slowly faded from sight in the west. The sun peeked through a shroud of haze, magnifying the entire sky with light. It was the seventh hour, and Weltheron woke to the sound of whining in the distance. This sound grew by the minute, meaning that whatever was making it wasn't far off. Realizing this, he didn't know what to do but hide his figure and by this become invisible. He feared the Raiders had come looking for him. Dragons had not only the ability to blend in with their surroundings but also exceptional vision. It was good for Weltheron that it was the morning, for almost the entire hillside was covered in the stuff he breathed, and the cold temperatures at night amid the mountains accounted for it.

Daring not to make a sound, Weltheron pressed slowly to the

ground, then watched and waited. A white animal soon appeared over the hillside and strode upon the green pasture, bending at first in one direction, then toward the other. This dragon-like creature bore wings but wasn't covered in scales. It rather bore a glossy mane and neighed. This animal was a white male pegasus, and he had come here to graze like he had done in the past.

Weltheron was ready to walk up to the pegasus and ask where he was but realized he might frighten the pegasus away if it saw him. Instead, he decided to ask this while he was still invisible.

"Pardon me," said the dragon. The pegasus, looking up with his ears perched high, gazed about. At first, he thought he was hearing things and continued to graze until the second time the dragon beckoned to him.

"Pardon me," came the voice again.

The pegasus, this time lifting his head, stood upright, ready to confront whatever was calling to him.

"Where are you?" he said, looking this way and that. "And *what* are you?"

"If I tell you, will you promise not to run if I show myself?" asked the dragon this time.

"That all depends," replied the pegasus. "What are you—some sort of wizard or Enchanter?"

"Neither," said Weltheron. "I do not want to harm you, but I'm looking for someone I can talk to without frightening him or her away."

"Why should anyone be frightened of you if you are friendly?" asked the pegasus.

"It's because I'm a dragon," admitted Weltheron, "and I must speak to someone." As he said this, he slowly became visible again.

The pegasus, seeing him, flinched but didn't flee. He stood and faced the dragon. When he adjusted a bit and saw the tameness of the beast, most of his fear left him.

"Who are you," asked the pegasus, "and where do you come from?"

"I am called Weltheron," answered the dragon. "I come from a hoard that lies far west of here. The reason I have ventured thus far is because I have just run away. I left on account that I do not fit in with my own kind. For one thing, I am the only white dragon in the clan, and for another, I am not a fire-breather. I make things turn rather to snow and ice. I am a frost-breather, and that is what they called me back home. I have just escaped my liege, Lord Glaider, who is out to kill me if I do not obey his bidding."

"Good gracious me," said the pegasus. "You *are* different, and that is disturbing to hear."

"Yes," remarked Weltheron. "But they will soon be out looking for me, and if they ever catch me, I will surely be killed."

"Oh no," replied the pegasus and wondered what to do. As he thought, an idea suddenly came to him. "If you are, as you say, an outcast, I know of someone who can help you."

"Really?" said Weltheron.

"Yes," said the pegasus. "I too am an outcast and dwell in a fortress, a refuge really, called Calivor. The master of this refuge is an old man, but he possesses certain powers unlike others. Excuse me for not introducing myself. By the way, I am called Starmane," remarked the pegasus. "I seldom come here to this pasture to graze, but now let me show you the way to Calivor. The way is hidden, so you must follow me."

Weltheron agreed, and with that, they both took flight, flying side by side and gliding in the wind. The day was underway, and Weltheron knew that right about now, trials had begun back at the Break. He wondered what his parents would think when they discovered he was missing. Would they be ashamed or sad due to his leaving? He also thought of what Glaider would do. He hoped nothing bad would happen to his parents on his account. He could only hope things would turn out all right. All this he pondered as he and the pegasus covered many leagues that day. Starting out, the sky was a flaming red and purple. Later in the day they encountered much fog, the kind where you cannot see anything in front of you, and you can get very lost.

"We are getting close," said the pegasus. "This kingdom is concealed by the great fog. My master devised it that way so no none can find it. Only I know the way, for I have made many flights and gone on many errands outside the veil." He said this as they were nearing the end of the fog's residue. Suddenly, the sky opened, and towering mountain peaks rose beneath them. In the distance, slowly coming into view, appeared the rooftops of a fortress, then an entire citadel. As they came closer, he and Starmane came to rest on one of these peaks to catch a clear view of the fortress's surroundings.

On what appeared to be a mountain shelf rested a magnificent palace, which measured almost as tall as the mountain slope behind it. "This is Calivor," remarked Starmane. "I have dwelt here since I was a pegaling. My master, whom you will meet soon, years ago rescued me after I was separated from my herd, which flew past the veil that conceals this refuge."

The dragon, gazing down on it, was filled with awe. The ancient stone structure had parapets and round spires reaching to the sky. He had never seen a man-made fortress before or any man-made thing for that matter. They flew down and landed in front of the fortress's gates, tall, rough-hewn planks bolted to a hammered iron support on top and bottom, with matching rounded handles. The walls and towers were built of limestone and the towers' rooftops; five of them were laid with slabs of flat stone to endure the harsh mountain climate. As they were about to enter, they were suddenly confronted by what appeared to be a winged elf. In Ëmerel-DUL, this people were too known as fairwings. This one that confronted them, was Uriel, who descended from one of the towers and was protector of the fortress gates.

He, like Starmane and Weltheron, was an outcast. Granted, he came from the Fairlands, an enchanted forest split into two that lay south of the world's map. The elf had been banished from his clan long ago on account that he was half human and half fairwing. As a sign that he was a half-blood, both irises of his eyes were different colors. One was olive green, and the other was royal blue. His long hair was straight blond, and his garments were fitted brown leather. These were fastened together with a black leather belt and a golden buckle around his waist. Upon his shoulders were grey leather pauldrons, which served as protection, and around his wrists were matching leather vambraces. For footwear, the fairwing strode about in oddly designed leather boots like the rest of his kind wore. He mysteriously wielded not a scepter but a normal man-made blade.

As his eyes fell on the dragon and the pegasus, he asked Starmane, "Why have you brought a dragon here?" He peered at Weltheron.

Starmane replied, "He comes in peace and is an outcast, the same as us, seeking shelter and counsel."

"I fear what the master will say when he sees a dragon," said the fairwing. "How do we know he isn't a spy, trying to learn of our whereabouts and secrets?"

"I stand by him," remarked Starmane. "He is no spy and begs audience with our master."

"Very well," replied Uriel, "but I must escort you in as protector of the fortress's gates."

The great doors were thrust open as the fairwing guided them in. The hall from within was vast. It had thick, round marble columns lining it from right and left, and it stretched back to a winding wooden staircase. Beside this flight of stairs to the right was a platform covered in smooth marble. It held a golden hewn throne, and on it sat a figure, who was the outcasts' master.

He indeed looked aged and had a long grey beard reaching down to his waist. His cloak and garments were neither decrepit nor shabby, but they were fit for royalty. His eyes, set back within a deep brow, were intense, with a hue of dark brown. Seeing the small party enter, he rose and stepped down to greet them. When he saw the dragon, an aspect of wonder grew on his face.

"Am I under one of my enchantments, or do I see a white

dragon?" he said. He came closer until he stood before the beast. Gazing at the dragon, his eyes found a mysterious mark riddled upon its forehead. It was a magician's sigil, and around this imprinted mark appeared a star, but in fact it was a glittering snowflake with eight arms, only its shape was in the radial pattern of stippling. The old man immediately identified the mark from that of an old friend. Such a mark, interpreted, said, "It is my will to protect and alter destiny." The true identity of such a mark could be seen only by noble eyes, which is why the dragon's lord had been blinded from seeing it.

"So it is true," responded the master. "Jack's hasty act didn't prove ill after all." When Weltheron and Starmane heard these strange words, they thought about what they meant and what was true … and who was Jack?

"Don't you realize," said the master, "that that which was foretold has come to pass? Amid the ever-burning stars like the sun has descended one, like this dragon, that bears such a mark on his head." Then the old man, drawing back his cloak, revealed from underneath a jagged and pointed object he wore around his neck on a chain. This was a bronze amulet, a lightning bolt with five points. His garments were somewhat majestic and were the hue of red scarlet, trimmed in silver design.

"I am the Weather Shaper, Casmin, one of the three Ëmerels," said the master.

"We are an order of magicians and keep a watchful yet unseen eye over this creation. As well as this, we possess certain powers that are dangerous and unpredictable, such as was carried out long ago by one of my order, who spoke the gravest of spells—that magic is strong enough to alter destinies, which explains why you, master dragon, are here. At first, I feared the other Ëmerel's hasty act would prove ill to the future, but today by some good fortune, fate has brought you here."

Upon hearing this, all were amazed and gazed at Weltheron, who now understood why he was different.

The Enchanter, staring at Weltheron, said to him, "What is your name, pale dragon?"

The dragon, standing silently almost the entire time, spoke for the first time. "I am called Weltheron, Weltheron the White, and I'm the only albino of my kind. I fled my home because of differences I couldn't mend and came here in search of answers. But you, magician, have answered all these for me, but still I have yet one more question to ask you. You say your kind sees everything that goes on. I wonder if you have ever seen a black and monstrous fire-breather before."

Then the dragon went on to tell Casmin that his clan was being oppressed by a nomad dragon named Glaider. The Enchanter was brought to distress about much of what the pale dragon told him. Many of these things puzzled Casmin, who, with his hands clasped behind his back, strode about the hall, deep in thought.

Once he had heard everything, he said, "All this is startling what you've told me, and I can say without any doubt that I have never heard of this beast until now. You said your kind never knew where Glaider came from before your kind came to settle in these parts?"

"Yes," replied Weltheron. "He is not one of us, and if you ask me, he is more a monster than anything. Since he has ruled my tribe, no one will stand to challenge such a terror as he, not even the strongest firedrakes, for they know the wrath of Glaider all too well."

"If Glaider is not one of you, as you say, master dragon, then who is he? Where did he come from? Why does he want to rule your tribe when he could easily rule these lands himself and not share the spoil from them?" These things Casmin pondered. "Is there anything else you can tell me about Glaider?"

Weltheron thought hard, trying his best to remember anything about Glaider that might prove helpful to Casmin. Then a thought came to him, or it was more like a memory that haunted him from when he had first encountered the monstrous firedrake. "One thing that does come to mind about Glaider was something he said to me before I defied the rule of the clan. He said I reminded him of someone he once knew. But there are no other dragons like me, as far as I know that is? Then this nomad said he would destroy them along with everyone else and fulfill his destiny."

Upon hearing this, Casmin was brought to utter silence. He looked as if he were stricken by a knife in the back. What ailed his mind was something he couldn't bring to the light before, but now he could see as clear as the day shone.

"It's him," said Casmin. "All this time I could not see it!"

"It's who? Who is it?" asked the few, besides Weltheron, who were gathered there.

"He is like me," replied Casmin. "He is Ganther the Concealer, one of the three Ëmerels, who now calls himself Glaider. My guess is, he has mastered the dark art of fire, wielding its magic inside him like that of a dragon, and he has transformed himself into a giant bat. All this must have happened after he altered his own destiny and became branded with such a helm's curse. And what better way to conceal all this from us Ëmerels than to hide away and lord over a race of beasts, masking himself to appear as one of them. It seems the age of dragons has come at last." Casmin uttered these final words in a hushed tone.

"If all this is true, then how has fate brought me here?" asked Weltheron.

"Because of that thing on your head," remarked the Enchanter, pointing at the dragon. "Such invisible marks my order calls Helms of Destiny, indelible ones. That power is channeled from the wearer's mind. They are a magician's desired outcome. The one you bear on your forehead, dragon, is the Helm of Ice and Shield. Its effects relinquish every ill thought, deed, and instinct in a creature. Not only can you master the forces of cold, for it is said in legend that if one who is a wearer of helms is found worthy, they shall also wield the Star Fire. It is not like normal fire and is so cold it burns. It comes from our creator, Semper, who is the highest power. He is the one who created the Helms of Destiny, and he is also the one who banned us Ëmerels from imprinting them on creatures for fear that they would alter life down the path of destruction. But all that has changed now because of you, Weltheron. Indeed, that which you think is your greatest weakness, pale dragon, may in time become your greatest strength."

"And what of Glaider?" asked Weltheron. "How is it that we are any different since both of us, as you say, were altered?"

"It is because Glaider bears another mark. His is the Helm of Fire and Dread," answered Casmin. "The effects of its magic stir up selfishness and greed in whoever wears it. Like the Helm of Ice and Shield, it is triggered by the mind, but instead it grants the wearer uncontested strength. It can strike fear into whoever gazes upon him or her, and it can summon every kind of evil that exists. One advantage, though, that you have, dragon, is that your magic helm has blinded Glaider's from detecting yours. It must have also caused forgetfulness since Glaider, once known as Ganther, is no stranger to wisdom. I assume you couldn't see his helm either. They are the mind's eye and can go unperceived whenever they deem. If Glaider hasn't unleashed such terror as he is destined to, it means he still must be building up his power and trying to understand such dangerous yet powerful magic himself."

"One thing you can be for sure of, too," said Weltheron. "My kind will not go on raids, for their holds are already rich with deposits of gold and gemstones, and they will rarely stir to leave them unguarded."

Upon hearing this, Casmin was relieved and concluded, "Well then, until then, master dragon, you must remain here, for I have other business for you to attend to. One more thing," added Casmin, raising a finger and striding toward Weltheron. "You say your kind calls you a frost-breather. Well, from now on, since destiny has brought you here, I only think it should be fitting that you be called … Winter Destiny. What do you think, master dragon?"

When Weltheron heard the Enchanter's suggestion, he became immediately taken with his new name and whispered it to himself over and over, repeating the words "Winter Destiny."

4

A COLD WELCOME

THE DAYS GREW shorter as time escaped. The hue of the grass and trees below the mountains slowly began changing from their original emerald-green color to golden yellow. Autumn had arrived yet again, along with an outsider who scarcely ventured from his cold refuge in the mountains. It was the Frost Master himself, who had come to meet his old friend, Casmin.

The two Ëmerels met on the plains of Durnhun, which on the map lay between the thrall of Maladron and the Barren Lands of Tybran. It was certainly an odd place to meet, but something was about to happen there that day that would sooner or later require their services. It was a vibrant day, and both Jack and Casmin arrived on steeds of their own—Casmin on his pegasus, Starmane; and Jack on his flying reindeer, Elibel. Unlike Starmane, Elibel wasn't a speaking animal; it was a she-reindeer. Despite this, Jack loved his reindeer and considered her his best friend. They both dismounted their beasts.

"Thank you for coming, old friend, or should I say, 'young friend'?" Casmin teased.

"You can have your fun once you tell me why you dragged me all the way down here from my home of bliss," said Jack.

"Something troublesome is about to happen, which is why I summoned you here. The weather should seem more fitting for you now that it is autumn. I apologize if it's not entirely like the winter you are used to all year round up near Stone-Cold Pass. It's been three years to the day since I visited you. Tell me, how are things and business at Snowflake Tavern?"

"Business couldn't be better. I'm thinking of adding an addition to Snowflake this coming month and hiring some more help. Thad, my innkeeper—you know him—is going crazy, and I have a lot of reading to catch up on from just assisting him in the demands of running an inn. But that isn't the only reason you dragged me all the way here to talk, is it? What troublesome things do you speak of that you say are about to happen?"

"Do you remember what we spoke of whilst in your concealed hall back at Snowflake?" responded Casmin in a low voice.

The Frost Master pondered in his already-cluttered mind what the Enchanter had brought to his attention. "Ah, yes, I remember," he said. "We talked about clans being at odds with each other, and one of our order had gone missing. What I remember most, though, was my hasty and foolish act. For years, I have kept a close and watchful eye on that dragon egg, hoping that nothing would go wrong. After it hatched and the creature grew older, I saw growth in him as well, a lack of satisfaction for the ways of his kind. This indeed was a positive sign for me, and I knew that the helm's magic was working. But the more I saw of what this creature had to endure, the constant anguish he was in day after day made me feel pity for him.

"It was as if this dragon was slowly being torn apart inside during the alteration. Just witnessing this from afar was more painful than if this dragon were terminated. Finally, I could not bear it any longer and tried lifting the spell, but after attempting to and failing, I realized such a spell could not be broken by others, as it is the Unbreakable Spell. It wasn't until a few months or so ago that I saw this rare offspring flying far from his hoard, as if having the intention of never returning. But then … everything vanished, and I could not see further as my power found its limit. I have nothing but a strong hunch that this dragon has fled his tribe because of differences that have proven too much for his own kind. I thought that maybe, just maybe, one dragon could change the rest. But I was wrong in even thinking such a thing was possible. I fear that I have made things more complicated. What it really comes down to is … you were right, Enchanter, in saying dragons would never come to change their ways." He let his head fall in disappointment. "I have learned a valuable lesson. I fear that my hasty act may have provoked our father, Semper, to turn his back on us."

"Stay your doubts for later, fellow Ëmerel," remarked Casmin, trying to cheer up his friend. "Hope is not lost yet, and you maybe have not changed an entire hive of dragons but still managed to change one. One is better than none, and who knows what fate will surprise us with because of it. We may now be only few, but wherever there are two or three of us gathered, there the spirit of Semper lies, even if his voice cannot be heard. What is done is done, and I promise you it has not been in vain. As for right now, all we need to be concerned about is the battle that is about to take place."

"Wait, battle! Did you say battle?" remarked Jack, suddenly perking up. He looked as if he were frozen stiff with his eyes and mouth wide open.

The Enchanter replied, "Yes, a battle is about to happen upon these very plains of Durnhun. The armies should be arriving anytime now. Can you make a snowball? I will need it to create something large."

"Hold on!" exclaimed Jack. "You can't just drag me into something just like that. This is not what I was expecting on a Saturday afternoon. Tell me, what's going on!"

"The clans that I spoke of before, that I mentioned were at odds, are taking things further and have gone as far as to start a useless war. We are here to stop them, and we will eventually need their help in stopping an even greater force out there. And you know of whom I speak, fellow Ëmerel?"

"But what of our order's rule of seclusion and secrecy?"

remarked Jack. "This generation cannot know that we exist unless our creator, Semper, says so."

"I see now you were not fooling when you said you have much reading to catch up on," stated Casmin. "If you've studied your history better, you would know it says in the *Book of Ancient Truths*, 'If there comes a time when peril becomes too dire, those of our order may intervene.' There is no time to explain everything, Frost. You must trust me. Now, did you bring your winter powers with you or not!"

The now-baffled Jack was out of excuses, and, slowly raising one of his hands, there appeared a snowball, which seemed to hover over them like a rotating globe. Already in the distance on one side of the Ëmerels, a great host of men and giants emerged over a hillside. All were clad in war gear and formed ranks in each army.

For the men, riding on a white steed was Lord Crestlin, son of Dillin, who wore a shirt of chain male and silver armor bearing the symbol of a black raven. It was the people's coat of arms and was branded on every flag, shield, and breastplate. The bird represented everything this people stood for and hailed before every banquet, and that was "Unity and Freedom." Apart from being a symbol, the raven was used as a messenger to bring word of happenings between the mother hall and sister halls. Maladron, where lived this race of mortal men, was a realm of many halls that lorded over surrounding settlements. There was Hedren hall, Kamor hall, and Ilard hall. But the one that bore supremacy over the rest was Hilgard hall. This was where Lord Crestlin resided, and the king had built a great earthworks around it to protect the mother hall from invaders.

The lord of men was helmetless, and his complexion was somewhat fair. He was in the prime years of his life, about thirty-four years of age, and he was lightly bearded, with long, dark-brown hair that matched it. The king's eyes were also brown, and he meant business by leading the houses of other lords in Maladron to battle. All Crestlin's knights, around seven thousand cavalry, were armed with swords and shields. The lord of men, too, brought with him two thousand infantry, most equipped with bows.

As for the giants, otherwise called "worlaugs," their chief, Andróf son of Fónó, rode before them. The brute sat astride a great rhino, his features stern and his hair dark and wild like an animal's mane. This people's skin was a shade of purple, and all were muscular and had long strands, like mohawks, lining the middle of their crowns and falling down their backs. All had donned animal hides, and their chief was likewise girded. Ropelike vine was fastened across his waist, used as a belt; and over this, he wore a crudely crafted garb of armor along with a rather large helmet. At the front of the helmet on either side were metal cheek pieces, and down the center of it ran a nasal bar to protect the brute's snout. There were at most two thousand in Andróf's army of giants, who strode afoot. All wielded crudely forged axes and bows, which were made from elk antlers.

This tribal race of giants dwelt to the east, amid the Barren Lands of Tybran. They were by no means fair or enormous, yet they still towered over normal beings. They tended to be somewhat troll like in look and stature. They didn't take pleasure in carrying out brutish behavior yet weren't the best at making friends. King Crestlin and Chief Andróf didn't look intimidated in the least by their opponents, an army of elves—winged elves, in fact. This force had arisen out of the South, on the other side of the Ëmerels, like a descending wall of cloud. They all landed amid Durnhun, each in a very organized manner, furling their wings once to the surface.

There were at least eight thousand of them. Helmondëm, son of Hedën, bore mastery over this people and their realm. They all wielded spear-headed staves, scepters that breathed magic, a magic that took the form of flame. But unlike red flame, this kind was green and wouldn't harm nature in the least—or anything good, for that matter. For every born elf grew one of these rods within their enchanted forest halls. These were gifts from their creator, Semper, since they were the first of many beings he had created. The fairwings' lord looked younger than those of his opponents, but in truth he was 12,093 years of age. His kind were also given the gift of immortality. The color of Helmondëm's eyes was olive green; the lord was arrayed in garments of majestic white, with a shirt of chain male over them. Over this he wore a breastplate that glimmered of iron-fetched silver, and upon his head was a matching metal diadem, which at the crest bore an emerald gemstone. It was both a helmet and crown, since it had two metal cheek pieces, yet it bore no dome on top. His vast wings, which measured as long as a condor bird, were as white as snow, and so were those of his kin. His long draped hair was the hue of gold, like the leaves of the trees that year.

Casmin and Jack watched the two forces observe one another for a while. It was obvious they didn't want war but weren't afraid to strike a blow to prove the other was wrong. Then like a dam being broken, the armies broke ranks, spilling over the plains and skies. A great cry arose, echoing throughout Durnhun.

The two Ëmerels stood out in the middle between both forces. The Frost Master, with his hovering snowball, was confused and nervously asked the Enchanter, "What is it that you were going to do again?"

Casmin, raising his hands and making a pose, replied, "Hold your snowball as still as you can." Then right before the Frost Master's face, the thing that could fit in the palm of his hand started to increase in size, so much so that it grew to be the mass of a thunderhead that now loomed from above. Casmin guided it over the ascending force of fairwings.

"Now, make it rain hail, Frost Master!" commanded Casmin.

A look of astonishment came over Jack's face, and he liked this idea very much. His eyes shifted to a cold white as the magic inside him was aroused. Then Jack, making his own pose, sent chunks of sleet falling from the sky onto the host of winged warriors. One after another, the fairwings were bombarded with hailstones, which sent them falling and staggering in flight, retreating to the ground. Once to the surface, they all used their wings to shield themselves from these massive chunks of ice. This step worked like a charm for Casmin and Jack, but now they had to deal with the men and worlaugs, whose armies were gaining ground from the north—and quickly. When they were within a half mile of the fairwings, the Frost Master beckoned the Enchanter.

"Now I know why you are otherwise called Weather Shaper," said Jack, "but what next, Enchanter?"

"Don't worry," remarked Casmin. "I have this all figured out. He will be here at any moment. Now to stop the men and worlaugs' charge."

"Who will be here at any moment?" asked Jack Winter anxiously.

As he said this, a large, pale dragon passed over them swiftly. The Frost Master ducked, putting his hands over his head, not knowing what was going on. Upon seeing the white dragon, he tried saying something to the Enchanter but couldn't since he was speechless.

"It seems that your hasty act did not turn out to be in vain after all, Frost," remarked Casmin. "Yes, that is the dragon you told me about and whom we now call 'Winter Destiny.' Watch him stop an advancing army with one breath and not harm a single soul while doing so."

As the dragon came around, he let forth a great breath like a snowstorm. This created a vast barrier of frozen ice to cease the men and worlaugs' pursuit. Once stopped in their tracks, the men and worlaugs were greatly confused. They couldn't put to words what had just happened, and all stood idle until some of them, who were among the largest and strongest of the worlaug army, tried hacking at the thick stuff with their axes. They all tried to break through its thick and frigid substance, but it was useless since the ice was so cold it was blue. The men's efforts were even less useful when they tried helping, and none of them could break through this mass freeze-over that now lay between them and the fairwings.

Jack Winter was beside himself. Putting his fists on his waists, he said to Casmin, "You knew about this? How is it that I was kept in the dark about it?"

"I was going to tell you, Frost, but that would've involved telling you something else that is of utter importance, not just to our order but to others."

"There's something else you didn't tell me?" asked Jack. "What is it?"

"Come, let us reason with our friends gathered here first," said Casmin, leading Jack by the shoulder out into the now-winter-covered plains of Durnhun.

It didn't take long for both rival forces to come face-to-face. Jack had hollowed an opening out of the mass freeze-over so the men and worlaugs leaders could meet with Lord Helmondëm. Both Crestlin and Andróf dismounted their beasts and passed through this vast barrier. All three lords were in stern moods but then again wondered who these two odd-looking men were who could summon such wrath on them. When all three of them were assembled, Casmin, who stood among them along with his comrade, Jack, immediately introduced themselves as magicians and Ëmerels. This greeting didn't take long, and Casmin, guiding the discussion, went straight to the heart of things.

"Lord Helmondëm and lords Crestlin and Andróf, I gather,"

said Casmin. "We apologize for such an unexpected intrusion, but we are here on a matter that far exceeds your differences. Held up in the Dark Mountain farther west of here, which sits amid the Claw, there has come to be a great hive of dragons. We do not know when they will beset these lands. You must all mend your differences and unite under one banner if we are to have a chance at stopping them."

Immediately, Crestlin spoke in bewilderment. "That mountain is cursed and has been vacant for years. Long ago dwarves used to make their mines up there, hundreds of caverns, in fact, that still exist to this day. This folk had discovered great wealth within the mountain, and at one time they held trade with my people in Maladron and in other kingdoms, but then they suddenly vanished from the outside world, and my kin and I never heard of them again. We suspected something had happened but didn't know what, and ever since, no one has dared to venture up there, for fear that they will meet with the same fate. If there are dragons as you say, magician, then how is it we saw a pale dragon fly overhead. And instead of unleashing fire on us, it breathed frost that turned to ice. What sort of new devilry is that?" asked the King.

"He is not like other dragons and is tame. You can say he is no friend of fire, as he is a frost-breather. You can thank my friend here for that," said Casmin, staring aside at Jack, "for it was he who infused his winter powers into this creature, and they are now manifest to the world."

"Since when are dragons tame?" intervened Helmondëm, who bore a look of disgust on his face. "They are all like these brutes and murderers who plague the lands afoot with their kind!" By this the fairwings' lord was referring to the worlaugs' kin, and at once this people's chieftain, Andróf, remarked in response to this harsh accusation.

"Hurorah," bellowed the worlaugs' leader. This was a grunting sound that all the gients made before they spoke. The chief worlaug lifted his hefty helmet from his head, revealing his features. His eyes were brown, his snout small, and his ears were large and sharp, the same as the elf. "We are not murderers!" he growled. "We hunt and kill to survive. We take what we need and spare what we don't."

"Did you spare my daughter, who went missing after your people and the humans saw fit to start a useless war?" retorted Helmondëm. "My scouts spotted your people near our forests not more than a fortnight ago. How do you explain that? Tell me, foe, where have you taken her?"

"Hurorah, I sent a couple of my people to spy on your woods' winged master," replied Andróf. "But they did not return with anything or anyone but word that something else was afoot within your realm."

"You lie!" snapped Helmondëm, who at that moment drew his enchanted weapon. He was about to use it on the worlaug, but another, drawing his own quicker, like a flash knocked the elf's scepter aside from his hands.

The one who did this was Jack, who amid the bickering had spawned an iced weapon of his own while no one was looking. He was smart like that but not one to challenge the might of a warrior like he had just done. This sudden intervention shocked Casmin and everyone else who stood there. Helmondëm was bewildered.

"This was something I thought I wouldn't have to use," added Jack bluntly, holding his ice-woven rod. "But I will if I have to!"

"Enough of this madness!" said Casmin. "Chief Andróf speaks the truth. Something else is afoot, and I know who they are, what they are, and why they have your daughter. They are shape-shifters, werewolves who dwell beyond in no-man's-lands. Their lair is a dark and cursed pine forest, called Werewood. It was at one time a place where mortal men dwelled, but now the castle is in ruins and has been deserted for hundreds of years. Long ago this people's lord had dabbled in dark magic and cursed not just himself but all his kin to brutes, and out of shame hid themselves in holes, caverns really, beneath their forest. Ever since, they've gone unbeknownst to man, but now they have emerged from the depths again. Their master is a hideous brute—Islarg is his name—but my order calls him the Murky Werewolf.

"It seems the dragons of the Great Treasure Hoard have formed an alliance with these bewitched men and their lord. Glaider is using them as his puppets to carry out his malice for him. Your daughter may yet be alive, but clearly this was done to cause waves between your people, Helmondëm, and yours, Andróf. And that is something that would please Glaider greatly, to turn you all against each other."

At this, the elf relented of his anger and spoke to the Enchanter. "If this is true, then where is your dragon now?" he asked.

"On his way to rescue your daughter, I presume," replied Casmin. "She will not be safe as long as the werewolves have her, for they are not just shape-shifters but flesh eaters as well. And once they figure out her kidnapping and this war are for nothing, her death is for certain. Our only hope now is the Winter Destiny."

5

THE TREASON OF GANTHER

THE SUN WAS setting in the west, its light escaping every mountain summit, all except one. And that one rose incredibly higher, with clouds hovering below it. It was the Great Treasure Hoard, and beneath the slopes of this shaded giant in a stone valley was a gathering of dragons. A great troop of them was perched on tall, spiked rocks pointed upward and scattered to and fro, but only one rested on the highest perch, and this one was Glaider. He and his brood of fire-breathers were expecting someone, and this kind traveled under the cover of dusk.

It was Islarg, and he arrived with a small pack of his fiends to discuss with the dragon lord matters of great importance. When he and his mongrels were not in humanlike form and appearance, they strode on all fours and howled and growled. Their furry manes were all dark grey and pale white, but only one was pitch black, and this one was Islarg. The irises of this alpha wolf's eyes were an eerie blue, and so were those of his pack.

It was the first of October, and there was a slight breeze that day. As these shape-shifters drew nearer to Glaider's presence, the Black Terror noticed they displayed signs of recent battle scars all up and down them, telling him something had gone ill. Islarg was the least bruised of his fiends and bore a look of fear on his face of how his liege lord would react to the news he had to bring him. "My liege, we came as swiftly as we could. We kidnapped the winged filth like you ordered, but later we were attacked—and not by theirs or any other kind but by one of yours. A pale dragon, he was, and he came like winter scorn, for he didn't breathe fire but frost that turned to ice and plagued our forest with it, turning everything stiff, including many of my mongrels. He took the fairwing and then flew south with her.

After hearing this, Glaider descended from his lofty perch, hovering over the wolf pack.

"Tell me, wolf man," said the dragon lord, who was curious. "You said he was white and breathed frost that turned to ice, did you not?"

"Indeed, master. He came out of nowhere, chasing many of us down, and swung his lizard-like tail round, casting us aside. We came at him from all directions, trying to penetrate this dragon's hide, but it was as thick as armor, and we couldn't pierce it. He and two others, magicians as I know it who wield strong magic, are the ones responsible for stopping the war below the mountains. One of my spies, whilst in human form among the ranks of men, saw theirs and the worlaugs' armies assailed by such sorcery as beset us in Werewood. They call this white beast 'Winter Destiny.'"

This news certainly angered Glaider, but what really triggered his rage was the name *magician*. The little that was left of Ganther in the dragon was now aroused. The black firedrake motioned his head back and forth as if trying to dismiss memories that were still there. But he was already caught up deep in thought and was swept back into the past.

The magician, Ganther, bore the appearance of a middle-aged man. His hair was black and not all that long though brushed back; his brows were quite sharp, forming a point. He was bearded also, only his beard wasn't nearly as long or as short as Casmin's and Jack's. His eyes were the hue of amber, and he wore golden earrings, crescent moons that matched his amulet. This larger object hung around his neck on a chain, the same as the other two Ëmerels. The crescent moon meant he could walk as seen and unseen by others. His garments were those of dark-grey leather, trimmed with gold design, and so was his cloak, which was hoodless.

Ganther had returned to his dwelling place, called the Hidden Cavern. He had come from a meeting with those of his order. Semper had spoken to the Ëmerels agian and had given Ganther a task. The creator sensed an evil presence in the land, but could not see it and bade Ganther to go and root it out.

Beneath a mountain slope, what appeared as rock face was only an illusion. Once passing through this phantom, the Shadow Walker entered what was his secret hall. From inside was hollowed in the ground, in the middle of it, a pool. But this pool was no ordinary dredge, for it was in truth a porthole into another dimension. The Shadow Walker called this pool his "cross-mirror." It was like Jack's frost-seer, but unlike other things, it allowed Ganther to enter the spirit realm, a self-contained reality, coexisting with Ëmerel-DUL. Only this version of the world was blurry and dull. It was here that the Ëmerel suddenly encountered a dark form, like a towering giant, that walked unseen to the physical world. Ganther, knowing it not to be Semper, fell on this outlander with his magic, but it was no match against the dark foe's, whose own proved stronger and this outlander cast a spell on Ganther, clouding the Ëmerel's reason. The foe then revealed to Ganther a destiny he couldn't resist. Ganther, overcome by pride, uttered the Unbreakable Spell, which went like this.

As he who utters this spell commits a treason,
Their daring to foretell,

As hidden as the night,
Farther than a person's sight.

As dangerous as a future holds,
You'll never know what destiny unfolds.

After the strongest of spells had been uttered, this outlander imprinted his mark, the Helm of Fire and Dread on Ganther's forehead. At the center of the helm was a sigil; this symbol was surrounded by a ring of fire, which encircled it and appeared as a seal. Such a mark, translated, said, "It is my will to inflict fear and summon evil." And this foe that had seduced Ganther gave him the name Glaider, a name he had used from thence. This was what he was known as, and he relinquished his humanlike form into that of a giant bat, which was what he remained ever since.

"They've found out!" snarled Glaider. "How did they find out? Who could've told them? No one knew of my scheme. They will die like everyone else!" he vowed in a vile and hideous voice. "And as for this white frost-breather, I will put his powers to the test with my own. I know who he is and remember fully his defiance toward me. He fled like a coward into the wild long ago. Tell me, Islarg, have my accursed creation awakened yet?"

The Murky Werewolf replied, "Yes, my liege, they grow by the day. The seven creatures have hatched from the black eggs you gave us. They have grown so large and fierce that my fiends and I were forced to bind them in chains. I fear they will bring ruin to our tunnels, which took us many years to construct. Our caverns beneath the earth are the only things that shield us from this world's scorn of light."

"Shadow will come over the land soon enough," stated Glaider. "You can stay your doubts for later, wolf man, for the very things you fear will destroy your lair will make this entire world your lair. And the sun will have little room to shine as its light will be blotted out by swarms of these evil beasts' offspring. It will not be long till these creatures of mine break free from your underworld. When this happens, you, Islarg, will invade Maladron and force the dragon out from hiding. I will send scouts to watch your every move and devise a plan to corner him so he cannot escape."

The dragon lord then ordered one of his fell birds to call a meeting of all the Raiders. This meeting was to take place in a secluded valley in the Claw, just a league or so from the Great Treasure Hoard. All the adults were summoned to this place, where none of them ventured often, for there was a reeking stench that came from there, for it was a hill made whole with heaps of bones from carcasses. It was called Skull Hill—a dragon grave site, it was; and it was used not only for the deceased but also for the disloyal in the clan. The Black Terror didn't mind thinning the herd if there were some who opposed him, such as Weltheron the White had done. A hidden fear rose in Glaider of this lone defiler, and he suspected he had been shown something by the two Ëmerels, but he didn't know what that was.

Glaider took his place on this mound, his gaze shifting about with a look of pride on his face. Then Glaider the Black began to speak. "My fellow Raiders, in the past I have been quite harsh. Many of you, I know, do not respect or regard me as your true sovereign, but do not quiver for I will not point you out. I rather come before you this day not to punish anyone but to bring you glad tidings. It is said in our law that any Raider should kill at all cost in order to gain great wealth. Yes, this is the law, but why seek wealth and haul it back to one place when there is power to be had? Why settle for countless riches when our kind can rule over this entire land? The other races cannot contend with us, and while we are among the greatest of birds to rule the skies, why not over kingdoms? If it means turning to ash a world that is old in order to make way for a new one, then so be it!"

Many of the Raiders gathered there agreed with Glaider, and others pretended to while listening to their lord. Among those who didn't share Glaider's vision were Weltheron's parents. Sëiron the Brown and Garthayn the Grey were beside themselves when they heard their lord talk of war and aught else. They were content with being Raiders and nothing more.

"There is something else I must tell you too," continued Glaider. "There has arisen in our midst a traitor, one of our own kind that long ago escaped and is now in hiding. As you are aware, our allies, the shape-shifters who dwell thither north, have met with this dragon's wrath. His allegiance lies with those who defy us with their presence below the mountains. I'm sure many of you remember that this dragon—a white frost-breather, he was—had a distaste for fire and defied the law of the clan. 'Winter Destiny,' they call him below the mountains. I want you all to find this traitor's lair and, once you do, report back to me, for he owes me a great debt, a debt he will pay with his life!"

Sëiron and Garthayn were dismayed when they heard this. Their dragon was the one Glaider had spoken of, the one he sought to find and kill. The two dragons didn't know what had become of their frost-breather, but they knew now that he was alive and safe in the company of creatures and beings the dragons neither associated with nor saw as friends. They had to warn their dragon before any of the Raiders got to him—and fast, for any day now there would come great calamity and ruin to the lands beyond.

6

MAKING AMENDS

U P IN THE hidden refuge of Calivor, the Enchanter Casmin summoned three of his friends, who were all outcasts. The lost Starmane, the banished Uriel, and the altered Weltheron were all gathered in the magician's hall. The dragon by now was an adult. He was fourteen feet tall when standing and eighteen feet long. He had a wingspan of twenty feet and was handsome for a male dragon. The magic from his imprinted helm had fully taken him over, so much so that certain aspects of Weltheron's face started to change over time. For one thing, a small line of stubs like ice horns formed down both sides of his temple, and under his chin, what looked like a goatee, were dripping fragments of icicles. Despite the dragon's increase in size, he still managed to fit himself in and out through the gates of the fortress, which were quite large as well. It was a tight squeeze but doable.

Casmin made Weltheron a scout, surveilling Calivor's surroundings and making sure no one besides those who dwelled there entered through the great veil of fog. When night covered the land and all were asleep, Weltheron rested outside the gates of the citadel, shifting in lucid dreaming. His kind called this "mind shifting," an instinct all dragons possessed when they slept while keeping a watchful eye over their spoils in case other thieving fire-breathers tried to steal them from them. It was one of the few instincts he still possessed, but instead of guarding treasure, Weltheron guarded his new home; that to him was more precious than anything else.

"I have seen something," said the Weather Shaper. "The skies with their cloud formations have revealed to me that a peace council has been called in the Fairlands by Lord Helmondëm. He has agreed to meet with the lords of men and worlaugs there." The Enchanter said this as he sat upon his throne. The rest of Casmin's subjects all stood in front of him, a distance back from his raised platform. One of them, Uriel, spoke up and asked Casmin, "Why does this concern us, Master?"

The Weather Shaper replied, "They will need our help as well as our counsel. We, master fairwing, all of us, are going there this very day, so you had all better be on your best behavior."

After he said this, Weltheron was about to speak when the fairwing spoke further. "But Master, I have not been down in those enchanted forests for years, and the lord of its keeping may object not only to the dragon's presence there but to mine as well."

"Your banishment should not make any difference now, fairwing. And if Lord Helmondëm has called a truce, then you and the dragon Weltheron must be a part of that truce. We are at war now, and it is about time we cast our differences aside!"

"But Master," pressed Uriel but was silenced by the Enchanter, who rose from his seat in his hall. "Whatever wrong has been done between you and your people must be mended when we reach the Fairlands." After Casmin said this, he then told all of them to be ready to leave within the hour, for the day was half over. and the sun was passing into the west. All three of them had flown together through the thick fog. Casmin rode upon his pegasus, Starmane, and Weltheron and Uriel flew side by side. The two of them talked some of the way to the Fairlands.

"What is the real reason you do not want to return home, if there is one?" asked Weltheron.

"It is a sad and weary tale," said Uriel. "The problem is not just that I'm half human and half fairwing. Long ago my mother, who was human, died when I was still young. My father grieved her death, which he didn't foresee. And once I was of age, because of how much I reminded him of her, he disowned me, banishing me from our realm."

"Then that only means one thing," said Weltheron. He was about to guess what it was when Uriel finished what the dragon was going to say.

"Yes, Helmondëm is my father. As of now, I do not know what he thinks of me, whether he still despises me or wishes he hadn't acted in such haste as he did."

"If you are the son of Helmondëm, then who is the fair daughter, the one I saved from the wrath of Werewood?" asked Weltheron again.

"She is my half-sister, Saylif," replied Uriel. "After my mother died, my father found love again. Only this time the one he wedded wasn't human but one of our people, and thus Saylif was born. She must be fully grown by now, and I still remember her as a child. Her hair and eyes shone as golden as ripened wheat and corn. Tell me, what happened after you rescued her from Werewood, dragon?"

"At first, she was afraid of me, but as I flew her back to her people in Durnhun, she began to stare and asked me, 'You are not like other dragons. How can this be?' I answered, 'And why would you say that, fair one?' Her response was, 'Because you protect rather than kill, and that makes you different.' This gladdened me inside," remarked Weltheron, who with a slight grin was brought to joy inside.

He and Uriel's conversation had come to an end since they were nearing the borders of the Fairlands. The four of them landed in front of the main entrance. The trees on either side of the path formed a unique arch over it, and all of them appeared to be blurry. The shield that contained this forest was a barrier of heat waves, circling round its perimeter. Inside the protected veil, the sun was shining, but outside the sky was an overcast of clouds. They could see their breath in front of them.

The Enchanter dismounted the pegasus and walked in front of the small band of outcasts. Turning and facing his companions, he said, "Before we enter these forest halls, we need to wait for one more. He will be here shortly."

Just as Casmin said this, a figure astride a gliding beast landed next to the small party. This, of course, was Jack Winter on his reindeer, Elibel. Gracefully the Frost Master, sitting on his enchanted beast, strode up to Casmin and the rest of them, saying, "Well, well, we all are here at last, it seems." Once he said this, he leaped off his reindeer, stroking its furry mane.

Jack strode up to the side of Casmin, and as he did so, he said, "Let me say, it is indeed the weather I enjoy most this time of year. Weltheron, it is good to see you again, my friend." At this, the dragon nodded in response to the Frost Master.

Casmin, crossing his arms, said, "I gather you are getting used to leaving your home of bliss now that there is a war about to happen."

"You know me all too well already, Weather Shaper," teased Jack. "Things have also started to slow down as far as business is concerned. The dwarf folk have become scarcer now, but there are some who are steady customers and practically live at Snowflake."

Weltheron, hearing this, bent his crown low and remembered what his kind had done to this people, whom Jack had spoken of. The conversation made him reflect back on when he had spared the dwarf's life during trials. These things Weltheron was reminded of and had trouble forgetting.

"Still no word of Semper?" Jack asked Casmin.

"No, nothing, Frost Master. I feel we are on our own in this one, seeing as how our kind provoked it. But do not take my words to heart the wrong way, old friend. If it wasn't for you, Ganther would have brought these lands to ruin by now, but it seems we have caused him great delay, and it has given us time to gather our strength against him."

As Jack was about to respond to the Enchanter's words, a great host of fairwings suddenly surrounded them all. All the elf warriors were clad in helm and armor. Their scepters were all raised above their heads, pointed at the small company. They all closed in from the ground while others were suspended in the air. They all bore fear in their eyes as they gazed on the white dragon.

Before Casmin and Jack, the fair people's ranks slowly parted, making way for one figure, who turned out to be Helmondëm. Like his kin the lord was clad in his war gear and bore a look of confusion.

"Greetings, Helmondëm, son of Hedën, lord of the Fairlands," said Casmin, bowing shortly. Seeing Casmin bow, Jack did the same but not as gracefully as he could have since he had been totally caught off guard.

"Why have you come here?" Helmondëm asked Casmin.

"It was you who called the truce between your people, the worlaugs, and humans," replied Casmin. "We are here to offer our help and allegiance."

With a scoff, the fairwings' lord answered Casmin, "Two magicians, a white dragon, a pegasus, and—"

At once, Helmondëm suddenly stopped and, peering over Casmin's shoulder, spied a familiar face, one he thought he'd never see again. The lord was in shock and, pacing between the two Ëmerels, strode over to Uriel, who only stared back at Helmondëm. When both of them were face-to-face, Helmondëm spoke again.

"I thought you were dead these many years, my son."

Uriel replied, "I thought I was already dead to you, Father. After my mother died, you grieved her death and pushed me away, banishing me from the Fairlands. I was given no scepter, such sacred staves that hold good magic, and was forced to steal a man-made weapon from Maladron. For many months I was without shelter and was a wanderer until I was found by Casmin and given refuge. Why, Father? Why did you push me away, and how did my mother die, and what was her name?" He said this in a groping tone of voice.

Helmondëm was at a loss for words. He was on the verge of tears and in response said, "It was out of guilt and mindlessness, my son, that I banished you. I feared you would blame me for your mother's death, for there is much you do not know. I still remember when I first saw her. She was tilling the soil, making ready for crops the humans grow during the warmth of summer and spring. She was the daughter of peasants I saw many times when I flew to Maladron on business with Lord Crestlin. Our eyes met every time. I still remember her face, which was fairer than any mortal I had ever seen before. Her hair was like the reddish foliage of oaken branch. Her eyes were as green as the grass that grows, and her smile shone like the sun.

"Back when the Fairlands traded goods with Maladron, our corn and other produce for their silks and precious jewels, I came before Crestlin and exchanged for many bushels of corn, enough to last his people many cold winters, I asked for this peasant girl in return. This Crestlin granted me since she had no family to call her own. Your mother's name was Nylund. Our love was inseparable, and when I bore her back to the Fairlands, I gave her to drink the Syculum Flower, a plant with petals that are the shade of sapphire. It is said that they hold a special nectar and that if one drinks, they will live longer than any mortal, and age will not touch them.

"After your mother conceived you, Uriel, her labor was so painful since her human body was not used to bringing a winged child into the world. She had lost a great deal of blood, and when all was over, so was her life. From that day on, I blamed myself for her death. As you grew older, my son, things were better, but then I saw a resemblance grow in you as well that in time spoke ill to me, and each time I gazed upon you, I saw your mother, and my heart became heavy. Then the day came when I could not bear it any longer, and in selfish haste, I banished you. I didn't even realize what I had done until it was too late. I felt as if a seducing voice had whispered in my ear, one I could not rid myself of. I regretted doing such a thing for many years and even tried finding you, but my scouts could not find any trace of your whereabouts and were forced to give up their search. I am truly sorry, my son, for everything. Please forgive me and know that there is still love for you in my heart."

When both heard each other out, there followed a long embrace and shedding of tears. This indeed was moving to behold. Once father and son were reconciled, Helmondëm out of gracefulness welcomed all of them into the Fairlands, including the dragon, and sought to reveal to them its hidden wonders.

7

THE FAIRLANDS

THEY ALL STARTED down a path through the thick forest. Once they entered the woodland, a warm front suddenly assailed the company. The weather dramatically shifted from cold to hot, and the newcomers no longer saw their breath in front of them. On either side of the path, sown from rich soil, were stalks of sweet corn, tomatoes, grasses of wheat, bean plants (which climbed the stalks), and every other kind of produce you could think of. It was as if this forest were a vast garden since everything there was not only trees and shrubs but also myriads of cultivated life.

This was how the fair people were able to survive many of the cold and brutal winters that occurred outside the shield. What is more, this safe haven teamed with life, including the chirping of birds and the buzzing of bees, all creating their own symphonies. The sun's rays peeked through the tops of the trees, casting light on everything that grew.

The Frost Master, despite the fact that he had begun to perspire somewhat from the warmer temperatures, was distracted from this when he spied large insects in that forest. They grew much bigger than those found elsewhere. What fascinated him the most were the monarch butterflies, which were arrayed in every color of the rainbow. They drew him in to inspect, but Casmin kept him from doing so and reminded him that they were only guests there.

It took the company several hours before they were almost to the other side. In the distance, one could hear the river rush, carrying on for miles and coming from the Stemming River. This fed off the coast of Ëmerel-DUL, making a channel through the Fairlands and dividing them into two separate woodlands. Upon reaching the riverbank, Helmondëm halted the company.

"Here, we will fly the rest of the way," he said. The Lord and his son had stridden together at the head of the company. "I just wanted all of you to witness for yourselves the splendor and beauty of the Fairlands, and I bid you all to respect and not hinder in any way all that grows here. Our halls lie yonder. Look, you can see them even now, hovering over the peaks of the trees for miles." The fairwing directed the newcomers' attention south.

Peering further in the distance, they could see what Helmondëm was pointing at. What looked like faint towers were vast trees— Magnums, they were called—which were larger than any other trees that grew in Ëmerel-DUL.

"Now let us go," said the elf lord, for the day is more than half over and there are those who await us." And with that, all the fairwings, took flight, escaping over the treetops.

Casmin and Jack mounted their beasts. Weltheron, flexing his wings to take flight, accidently created a strong gust of wind, surging down the path they had just come from and shuddering trees and plants alike. The dragon cringed when he realized what he had done.

Jack, who had not yet departed, looked back at the forest, then at Weltheron, laughing at the dragon. "Wind is good. It's healthy for nature. Let's go, or we'll late," he concluded, urging his furry-antlered reindeer on.

Casmin was already gone, and Weltheron was last. Looking back at the trees, the dragon thought for a moment, then quickly lifted off the ground and followed the rest of them. He had to make up for falling behind and climbed higher to catch up. Once up close with the Magnum trees, the dragon was taken back with awe. There were four of these giants of the forest, towering one thousand feet high; each trunk was thirty yards wide. All of them were covered from top to bottom with thick moss and had bark similar to beech, and their leaves were the color of marigold flowers, all glittered when the sun's rays fell on them. The two magicians and dragon landed on a clearing a few yards from where the deep-rooted Magnum trees stood.

This glade was surrounded by Helmondëm's warriors, and they had kept an eye on the beasts as their masters went thither to the great hall of their Lord. However, from among the warriors was someone who recognized the dragon. This turned out to be the princess, Saylif. The fairwing had emerged from nearby oaks, not expecting to see her rescuer again. She was crowned with a headdress of leaf and flower, lilies, which glistened of lilac pink. Saylif was clad in ornate garments of silver, like a tunic of leaves strewn together.

When Saylif spied the dragon, she remembered when the werewolves had taken her. It had been near dusk, and she had strayed as far as the second forest when scouts of her father had met her—that is, until those foes relinquished their masked forms. Those accursed men had the ability not only to transform into brutes but also to clone other creatures' looks and appearances.

They seized the princess and bit her the arm, imbuing a venom, which caused Saylif to fall into a deep sleep. She slept for nearly three days, and when she awoke, she realized she was deep in the forest of Werewood. There she was surrounded by countless fiends, which looked hideous at first sight. Many of them spoke of feasting on her arms and legs, but some mongrels in charge protested, saying, "No, not until Islarg says we can! We must wait until the war begins between our enemies. Then we can feast."

But then the white dragon showed up, raining thick snow and sleet down on that eerie forest, turning many of these beasts stone cold. Indeed, she hadn't forgotten this noble deed and made it her intention to speak to this tame dragon again.

She sought to slip past the guards surrounding the perimeter, but before she could, one of them stopped her. The guard caught her by the arm and, pulling her aside, said, "Are you mad, princess? That monster would snatch you up quicker than we could stop him!"

"He's not a monster!" remarked Saylif, trying to wrench away from the guard's firm grip. "He's my friend, and he is the one who rescued me from our enemies."

The guard, confused by the girl's strange remark, gave her a baffled look and replied, "Your friend? Dragons are not the friendly type. They know only deceit and terror. He may be an ally of our people, but that doesn't change what he is, your grace."

Saylif, almost brought to tears, freed her arm, turned about, and flew back to where she had come from, toward the giants of the forest. Helmondëm and his son, along with Casmin and Jack, entered one of these tree giant's halls through a large hollow, which opened up at the base of the tree. This bore no gate, and this people didn't need doors, same as they didn't need stairs, for they were always mobile and didn't like to be shut away. A beam of light shone through this void, pouring into the hall, which lay within.

Once they were inside, the odor of wood filled the air. It smelled like lavender and was very soothing, and every Magnum tree gave off this scent. The floor of timber was riddled with a radial pattern of rings, representing the tree-giant's life span, which ranged from thousands upon thousands of years. Then the two magicians, Casmin and Jack, turning their gaze upward and saw a lofty city looming from above. There were hundreds of uniquely shaped houses, the structures of which were similar to those of cocoons. All of them rested on wooden planks running up and down the interior and lining the walls from top to bottom. The vast interior echoed with life and the stroking of wings as the fair people went about their daily routines. It was like a whole new world from inside, and the upward climb of one of these trunks seemed almost endless from below. In a place this vast, one would assume it was lit by torchlight, but flame wasn't what this people used. They possessed something else that in great multitude produced light of their own. This light came from fireflies living inside the halls, and they were not irritating in the least. There were thousands of them, all illuminating like stars.

From below, half the company had gathered around a miniature-sized tree stump, which stood in the center of the room. This wooden stub was used as a table, and spread out on it was a charted map of Ëmerel-DUL. Already standing around this platform, enticed with maneuvers of war, were lords Crestlin and Andróf. As part of the truce, Crestlin had come there by himself as well as Andróf. It was a two-day ride from Maladron to the Fairlands. The worlaug, unlike the human, had traveled on foot since his kind were swifter this way, and both had arrived around the same time. It was only a few hours later when Casmin and Jack showed up, along with Helmondëm and Uriel, and all joined in the discussion.

Now the lord of the Fairlands was glad that the two magicians were there to offer their counsel, for when it came to the topic of Glaider, it changed their whole strategy. This monster didn't just breathe fire; he possessed powers these forces of beings couldn't contend with and looked to Casmin and Jack to give them advice. "What has come to my attention from Winter Destiny," said Casmin, "is that the dragons guard the Great Treasure Hoard, which is why they have not beset these lands. But once the hive has reached its limit and cannot house more offspring, then this is when we have to worry about Raiders coming down from the mountains. As well as all this, my friend, the Frost Master and I have seen something, another kind of evil, that has been awakened in the land."

8

THE BATTLE OF MALADRON

"WHAT ARE YOU talking about? What have you seen?" asked Crestlin. The lord of men looked confused and worried, and so were the rest of those gathered in the great hall.

"There has come to be a new kind of threat to the land?" remarked the Enchanter. "This one has arisen out of the North, where the thrall of Werewood lies. It seems that Glaider has finely unleashed his dogs."

Crestlin's face became pale and started to perspire. His realm lay closest to these fiends' lair, and if such menace could infiltrate the Fairlands under Helmondëm's watch and kidnap the princess, then it most certainly could do so in Maladron. But this wasn't the only thing that terrified him, for back at Hilgard he had a family, a wife and son he now wished he hadn't left. His wife, the queen, was called Laylath, and their son was named Orthalin. Crestlin's son, quickly coming of age, was nearly thirteen. Every worst possible thought filled Crestlin's mind, and he feared that his leaving Maladron leaderless had been a grave mistake. Without thinking, he was about to storm out of that vast hall when suddenly his friend and ally Helmondëm caught him by the shoulder, beckoning him to stop. "Wait, wait, Crestlin!" he said. "If what Casmin says is true, then it means you will meet with more resistance than you can put down."

"And what if there are hundreds of these shape-shifters?" replied Crestlin. "They have not seen the strength of Maladron or the might of Hilgard's walls. We will put their strength to the test with our own. There is no time to waste. I must go now!"

"Hear me further, lord of men!" begged Helmondëm still. "What I mean to say is, maybe these shape-shifters are not the only things your people have to worry about."

"He's right," intervened Jack, who for the most part had been silent when it came to talk of war. The Frost Master stood alongside Casmin at the table, with his hands resting on its flat surface. His head was bent as he surveilled the map. Jack, slowly lifting his crown, stared at Crestlin and finished what he was saying. "You may meet with more than teeth in this fight. If Glaider has by now mastered such power as is dangerous, he can bring to life greater evil than what Werewood is capable of and is using these fiends to steer such menace to where he will strike first. Something worse is at play here, and unlike normal dragons, this kind is bred for war."

"And what are you saying then—that I should just forsake my kin, my family?" remarked Crestlin, peering from one person to the other. "I'd rather die than cower from such odds as are against me."

"No one is telling you to desert your people or your family," said Helmondëm. "If Glaider has spawned another kind of dragon, then you will need my help, friend. Our scepters that we wield, that breathe good magic, are just what we need. On top of this, we have the two magicians, Casmin and Jack, to help us. We will need all the magic we can muster to stop an enemy such as this ... It is time that we fight as allies again, my friend!"

"Hurorah, we fight!" roared Andróf suddenly. Once hearing his friends out, Crestlin was now more inclined to except their help. "We must hurry then, for the enemy may already have a head start on us," said the king. "I cannot take my steed. It will be too slow, and I will certainly push it too hard to make it back to Maladron on time."

"Then you will ride with me," responded Casmin. My pegasus

can carry more than one person. Chief Andróf, you will ride the dragon. He can carry about your weight."

"Hurorah!" said Andróf. "I will ride the dragon back to Maladron!"

"Come then. We must leave now," said Casmin, and with that all of them started for the glade outside the hall. Casmin and Crestlin mounted Starmane, and Andróf mounted Weltheron. The worlaug held on tight to the spikes lining the dragon's back. The Frost Master, Jack, taking hold of his reindeer's antlers like he always did, flung himself up on to its back. This he could do since he was light footed. Helmondëm and Uriel led a host of six thousand of their kin, all armed with scepters. Then, like a rush of wind, they all departed for Maladron. For many hours they flew, passing over forests, rivers, and grasslands until reaching the outer borders of Crestlin's kingdom. As they entered the realm, they all spied a darkness in the distance, knowing something was already looming in the lands beyond. There was still light left in the day, but it was fading quickly.

Farther north, a thick blanket of shadow was descending over a line of mountains that divided Maladron and no-man's-lands. Only there was a passage that ran parallel to the Slithering River, creating a channel through the mountains. In the distance could be seen smoke and fire as a multitude of dark figures made their way into Maladron. These no doubt were werewolves and at first glance looked like hundreds, which later turned out to be thousands. Countless howls echoed throughout the open plains, the sound carrying on for miles. Many of these ascended from the location of the halls of Hedren and Kamor. Crestlin guessed that these halls were already overcome and laid waste. Luckily, Hilgard and Ilard halls were untouched, but they would soon meet with resistance like an oncoming storm. Both opponents approached like two massive waves quickly advancing; resounding cries and blows rang throughout.

The first to leap into action was Andróf. The giant leaped from the dragon's back as they neared the ground, and with one stroke, he smote a throng of werewolves with one of his battle axes. Uriel and Helmondëm's hosts fell on these brutes more quickly than a person could blink. Many of the fiends leaped at the fairwings, tussling with them to the ground. The son of Helmondëm, with honed scepter, cleaved two shape-shifters in half and scorched several with surging blasts of magic. Many of the mongrels didn't know what was going on; all they saw were other fiends being hit with beams of green flame, and many of them became frightened.

Weltheron soared high and circled around. As he approached the ground, he came face-to-face with beastly creatures, seven total, called fiend-breathers, concealed by an overcast of dark haze. Their eyes burned like balls of flame. They appeared as giant serpents, crawling about on their stomachs, and their scaly hides were pitch black. The resounding bellows of each were loud enough to make the ground shudder like an earthquake. As Weltheron approached, one of these foes opened wide its cavern, spewing not flame but dozens of creatures. "Drats," they were called, a crossbreed between dragon and bat, who in turn breathed blue flame of their own.

The white dragon, seeing them coming in great numbers, sent a frigid blast, stopping the creatures in their shuttle. Many of the drats were frozen instantly. Hundreds fell from the sky on those below, crushing good and bad alike. Weltheron soon found himself overwhelmed as each of the seven fiend-breathers unleashed unrelentingly.

Casting aside a werewolf's carcass, Helmondëm realized there was a fight going on from above. He saw Winter Destiny being overwhelmed, and with a multitude of his kin, he rushed to the dragon's aid. After shooing their mounts away, the two Ëmerels fought side by side, cleaving, hacking, freezing, and striking werewolves coming at them from all directions. The Weather Shaper released bolts of lightning from his hands, scorching masses of beasts at a time, and Jack spawned two frozen weapons shaped like maces. Whack! Whack! In every direction, they were slaying fiend after fiend.

Now Crestlin became concerned about his people, most of all, his family back at Hilgard, and once locating the two Ëmerels, he ran toward them as fast as he could. Amid the chaos, Crestlin had beckoned the Enchanter to summon his pegasus so he could ride it back to the fortress. The Enchanter, busily fending off werewolves, remarked, "Do you think I can just call my steed back like that? He is long gone until this battle subsides!"

"But I need to get back to Hilgard! I need to find out what is happening there. It is more than several miles afoot, and I fear my kin are in danger," remarked Crestlin.

Jack, overhearing Crestlin and Casmin's conversation, suddenly perked up. "I think I can help you, lord of men," he said. And without warning anyone, he sent a shrill-like whistle so loudly through the air that it stunned everyone there, including the shape-shifters. All their ears rang, but the beasts' lobes were even more sensitive, and many of them fell, groping the ground.

A distance off, away from the fighting, grazed Jack's reindeer. But once it heard her master's call, she knew to return to him swiftly. Upon her arrival, the battle was waging again, and Jack, after embedding one of his weapons into a brute's skull, went and helped Crestlin mount his reindeer. Crestlin, unlike Jack, couldn't swing himself up on its back and needed a boost. Once this was done, Crestlin held on tightly to the beast's mane; and with a kick, it was off before Jack could tell him how to ride it.

The shape-shifters grew all the more angry and came at the magicians in overwhelming droves. There were so many that the Ëmerels were surrounded by packs of them and bore little room to even breathe. When this happened, Casmin and Jack shape-shifted themselves. Casmin became as a twister, sucking up dozens of brutes and sending them hurtling through the air. Jack turned into a frost giant, and despite having dozens of mongrels amassed on him, he was impenetrable. Both of them, Casmin and Jack, made such a stand singlehandedly that once the werewolves realized they were no match against them, they retreated, scurrying back in the direction of the mountains. There were heaps of bodies everywhere, all mostly brutes. Andróf and Uriel pursued the werewolves as they fled, doing their best to route them. While all this was going on from below, a mile north from above, Weltheron and Helmondëm were having trouble trying to resist the fiend-breathers. All seven of these monsters sent waves upon waves of drats—and not only at the dragon. But swarms of them came at the host of fairwings, killing many until the only one left was Helmondëm. The elf didn't possess armor like the dragon and started taking heavy blows from cuts to burns until he himself was being swarmed. Seeing Helmondëm in danger, Weltheron thought desperately about what to do despite the fact that he himself was being assailed.

Then, shutting his eyes, Winter Destiny turned his thoughts inward. When he did this, everything around him suddenly faded. The magic inside him was aroused, driven by his will to protect. The imprinted helm on his forehead began to morph into what one could say was a black hole, and from it shone a dazzling light like an aurora, beaming up into the atmosphere and drawing forth a mysterious energy. Like blood rushing through veins rushed the coldest and hottest of matter, the Star Fire. It burned hotter than any fire known to man and colder than any ice. Weltheron in agony was somehow able to withstand this intense infusion. Once the matter filled the dragon's entire being, he was transfigured as if into a light, so bright; it resurrected almost the entire land of Maladron from darkness. With his eyes now open, he turned his piercing gaze on a now-bewildered enemy.

The drats that had once swarmed him and Helmondëm were now crippled with fear. Winter Destiny unleashed a torrent of Star

Fire, which shone like a glittering dust of golden white; one by one it dissolved the drat creatures and fiend-breathers alike. Not one of these foes could withstand such force. Winter Destiny purged these dark forces of evil from the land. It wasn't until the dragon spewed his last breath that he relinquished his bright form and returned to his normal shade of white. Thick shrouds of smoke and stench had risen from the plains. The dragon, once retreating to the surface, met Helmondëm.

The lord, spent from battle and riddled with the blood of his enemy as well as his own, strode up to the dragon. Breathing deeply, he spoke with awe. "You never cease to impress me, Winter Destiny. You are indeed an unpredictable dragon." Once he had said this, the two Ëmerels suddenly showed up.

"Are you all right, Weltheron?" asked Jack. "I thought the world was coming to an end, but now I see I was mistaken. You have gotten Semper's attention, it seems. You've harnessed the Star Fire, something no one has ever done before. Only a wearer of helms that is found worthy can do this."

Weltheron was exhausted. He was still dizzy from absorbing the Star Fire, whose fatal and burning matter nearly cost him his life (and while trying to stomach it, he had done all he could to keep from exploding).

"Where is Crestlin?" asked Helmondëm suddenly.

"He went back to Hilgard. He said he was worried about his kin, which reminds me. I need to find Elibel, my reindeer," replied Jack, suddenly realizing he had loaned her to Crestlin.

"I had better go with you Jack, just to make sure everything is all right," said Casmin. "Can you fly us back, Winter Destiny, or are you still regaining your strength?"

"I've never felt better" were the only words Weltheron uttered in response.

9

WARNING SIGNS

CRESTLIN, RIDING JACK'S reindeer, was nearly to the fortress of Hilgard. Its vast walls, built of stone, harbored a great village. The battlements formed a great sphere around them. The king, astride his enchanted beast, once ascending over the barrier, was bewildered to see multitudes of bodies. All were slain warriors and fell beasts, shape-shifters whose carcasses slowly relinquished their masked forms. Continuing even below the defense were men, women, and children lying up and down the village roads. There were puddles of blood everywhere. They all formed a trail of corpses leading up to Hilgard, which rested on a hill overlooking the town.

Seeing such death, Crestlin stirred his beast on more quickly. He finally landed amid a stone terrace outside the hall and quickly dismounting, he then shooed his animal away. Finished, he tried pushing open the citadel's wooden doors, which were made of solid oak, but they were bolted from the inside. Crestlin then gave a loud knocking, beckoning anyone to open the gates and proclaiming that he was the king who had returned. It was only after he did this that the doors slowly parted, and from them appeared four knights, captains who greeted their king. They all looked dismayed and surprised when they saw their master. One of them immediately spoke.

"My king! We've been waiting for you," said one called Antar.

"We didn't know when you would return. The fortress has been taken, and we were forced to retreat back to the hall. Did you come alone, my king?"

"Yes, I am alone, but alas, what has happened here, Antar? I saw slain knights lying in great numbers. I too saw fallen fiends. A handful of them managed to scale these walls. I wish to know once I hear that my wife and son are safe. Pray tell me. Where are they?" asked Crestlin.

"Do not worry, O king. They are safe. We defended them from those who attacked and killed them. It is good that you are here now. Come, follow us. We will bring you to them!" said the captain as he and those with him turned to walk back inside the hall.

As Crestlin was about to follow them in, he spied two fallen warriors lying beside the gates, but both looked identical to the men he'd spoken to. This resemblance astounded him, and he was even more taken back when he saw that they also wore the same clothing and bore the same head of hair. Their faces were covered in soot and blood, and so was their war gear. The ones who had confronted Crestlin weren't in the least covered in waste that would have come from a fight.

Once seeing this, Crestlin smelled a trap. Before walking any farther, he pressed the guards striding before him. "Soldiers, where are your battle scars? You said you helped defend this hall. If what you say is true, then at least show me your blades, for they must certainly tell a diffcrent tale."

Stopping and hearing these words, the guards for a moment said nothing. Then one of them slowly turned and began to take on another shape and form. The others eventually did the same, and now before Crestlin stood four ugly and furry beasts, whose eyes burned with hate. "You think you are wise, human?" one said. "You are one man against four of us mongrels, who singlehandedly ripped to shreds the defenders of this hall."

This was Islarg who taunted Crestlin. Upon hearing this, the king's sword leaped from its scabbard, and with a cry he charged these four foes head-on. Three of them bounded at Crestlin and did their best to avoid the lord's flailing weapon, but one of them couldn't since Crestlin was a master of the sword. He slid under these beasts, guiding his blade down the stomach of one. The wolf screeched in pain, then fell lifelessly on the stone terrace. Gore ran from its body, a puddle of it emerging from beneath its carcass. Then a second Crestlin put to the sword and then a third until only Islarg was left.

The alpha wolf was larger than those of his brutes. From his mouth dripped saliva, much of it still the hue of red from feasting on man flesh. Islarg bounded beside the balcony, blocking the steps leading down. He sought to back Crestlin into the hall to kill him. The werewolf's eyes glowed in the dark, and the hair on his back stood upright. He was about to lunge at Crestlin when suddenly something yanked him from behind. This turned out to be the dragon, Weltheron, who appeared from beneath the stone porch. The dragon dragged the werewolf down by its tail. The shrieking alpha tried to resist with all his brute strength, dragging his diggers and riddling the slats of limestone.

Casmin and Jack sat astride the dragon. Jack alighted the dragon and attended to Crestlin, who was in a fury and still wanted to slay Islarg, but both magicians wanted to send a message back to Glaider. The Frost Master immediately froze Crestlin in one position so he couldn't move.

Weltheron threw Islarg on his back and held him down, not allowing the beast to move an inch. Casmin, leaping off the dragon, at once questioned the Murky Werewolf. "Your master, Glaider, sent you, didn't he? We know who he really is and what he plans to do. Go and tell your master he has lost the battle of Maladron and that Semper has anointed a Helm Wearer, worthy of the Star Fire."

After Casmin finished, he motioned to the dragon to release the werewolf. Islarg sprang to his feet and scurried away as fast as his legs could carry him, passing through the fortress gates Casmin opened for him with a burst of wind. This brute headed for the Great Treasure Hoard, daring not to look back in case the magician changed his mind and had him killed instead. Darkness filled that land, along with much lamenting from the battle. Crestlin's wife and son were found scattered in pieces inside the mother hall, and greatly Crestlin mourned their deaths.

The royal family was then buried beneath Hilgard in crypts under its fortified mound, eternal resting places for lords and nobles of that house. The only citizen of Hilgard still alive was Crestlin, but he wasn't without kin to lord over, for further west Ilard hall still stood. Their people bore the mark of the griffin since they were known to be a fearless clan, save for their lord, who was called Norghoth, but he was in truth a coward. During the battle of Maladron, the lord had ordered the sentries of his hall to bolt shut its gates. Not only had he not taken part in the fight, but he'd abandoned his people, the one thing he had sworn never to do. This news angered Crestlin, who held supremacy over Norghoth; once learning of this, out of mercy, he banished Norghoth from Maladron into the wild.

The great fiend-breathers had destroyed the halls of Hedren and Kamor and their surrounding villages. After Norghoth was dethroned, his people moved to Hilgard to take shelter behind its walls, and from thence, they lived under the sovereignty of Crestlin. There was no point in rebuilding the ruined halls north of Hilgard, for there would come a day now when another threat would come over the land. This no doubt would descend from the vast and menacing-looking mountain lying to the west.

Winter Destiny and the two Ëmerels didn't leave Maladron suddenly after everything had happened. They remained in Maladron to ensure the safety of their people. The fairwings and worlaug, however, needed to return to their dwellings to muster the rest of their armies. Now everything would come down to one final battle, and this was something no one was looking forward to, especially Weltheron, knowing he would soon come head-to-head with the Black Terror. Indeed, it would be some time till the Raiders came down out of the mountains again, but why wait for that to happen? They decided the only thing left for the rest of them to do was to take the fight to Glaider and destroy the hive once and for all, but this wouldn't be an easy task.

A fortnight passed, and King Crestlin expected the return of both of his allies. It was the first hour of the morning, and the moon shone brightly in the kingdom of men. Everyone was still asleep in Hilgard save Weltheron, who rested several yards outside its walls.

Clouds loomed overhead, casting shadows and moving about like ghosts in the night. As the dragon half slumbered, he noticed a strange cloud moving swiftly across the sky. This caused him to become fully alert and awake. Weltheron soon realized this wisp of cloud was a dragon, and it landed several yards away, touching down on the surface. It then quietly and boldly advanced toward him.

The pale dragon was prepared to make a stand but didn't know whom he was about to confront. Had Glaider come to challenge him? Then slowly rising from his bed, the albino let the intruder know he was seen and advanced, staring down this Raider, who was nothing except a shadow. Even as timid and tame as Weltheron appeared, he wasn't to be trifled with as he had proven in battle. Like a bull before it charges, Weltheron exhaled deep breaths of steam from his nostrils. The opposing dragon continued advancing yet was still too dark to identify.

It wasn't until both dragons came within striking distance that Weltheron suddenly recognized the other dragon. "Sëiron, my father. Is it really you?" said Weltheron, who looked confounded. "What are you doing here, and how is my mother, Garthayn, your mate?" he asked.

At this, the other dragon, Sëiron, replied, "Your mother is well and is back at the hive, guarding our claim. I flew here once learning that Glaider's attempt to overtake these lands was a failure. The shape-shifter you spared returned to the hoard and spilled the truth to Lord Glaider. He had gotten no further than telling him you and other forces had prevailed when Glaider without hesitation devoured this mongrel and went into a fury. He wants you dead now more than ever and won't stop until you are hunted down and killed, my son."

"Have you come here to warn me or discourage me?" asked Weltheron.

"Mainly to warn you, my son, and to tell you that most of the Raiders are against starting a useless war," remarked Sëiron, "and for what purpose? The great hive already holds countless spoil, and there are at least two more cycles of offspring to be born before another hive can be started. There is much unspoken frustration and fear in the clan."

"And what do you think of this, Father?" asked Weltheron. "Would you stand by and let Glaider make a hive of Raiders into monsters?"

"To this world, we are nothing but monsters. Our kind will never make peace with those beings you call your friends. I fear the only friend we will ever know is the wealth we possess. But tell me, who is Glaider really, for we both know that such a living terror as he couldn't have been bred by any such spawn of dragon?"

"If you already know that, then there is no harm in me telling you," said Weltheron. "The one who calls himself Glaider is in truth a sorcerer, called Ganther. He is like my master that I serve, who is amongst an order of three."

"So that is it, why Glaider seeks to change our ways and make us adapt to his own. And what of you, my son? How is it that you are different yet were born as one of us?"

"The other member of the three, whose name I didn't mention before, is the one responsible for making me the way I am. Jack Winter is his name, and he also is a bearer of frost, same as I," said Weltheron. "The mark on my forehead that spoke wonder to you all these years has turned me from my former ways. It is a magician's sigil, and its magic is strong enough to alter destinies. They are otherwise called Helms of Destiny." Then Weltheron went on to tell his father, everything he felt inside, that he could not find the words to spell out for him before.

A dragon I am, a Raider you sought,
But this was not so, as destiny wrought.

A dragon I am, fire you thought.
My scale was white. My breath told you naught.

A dragon I am, of wealth I was taught,
But this did bring me heft, only aught.

A dragon I am, a bearer of frost.
I doubted my worth, my pride all but lost.

A dragon I am, Glaider I crossed.
I fled from my home in search of a cause.

And found I was seen, for who I was.

A dragon I am. I'm not at a loss.
I know who I am, though you might call me dross.

My quest is all but over till I fulfill my destiny.
This, can't you see?

A dragon I am. This I can't change.
I bear it inside me, like an ill mange.

As timid as a lamb, you might call me a shame,
But I know what I am; alas, a dragon I am.

10

A BARGAINING

ONCE THE DRAGON finished explaining everything, his father, Sëiron, asked him, "And what is your destiny, my son?"

Weltheron, replied, "To face the Black Terror and bring his malice to an end!"

"What are you saying—that you alone can overthrow Glaider? That is madness. You would be torn to shreds and left as prey for the vultures."

"I do not know if my powers are even strong enough to overthrow him, but I must try for the sake of others who have endured this monster's reign long enough."

Sëiron, bending low his crest, sighing as if in disbelief said, "If you think you are going to face this nomad alone, then you are wrong, my son. When you do, I will be there, standing by your side. But tell me, frost-breather—or should I say Winter Destiny?— when will you come home? The longer you wait, the more powerful Glaider grows each day."

"This I know, but I must wait till my master orders me," said Weltheron.

"Come back now, my son?" beckoned Sëiron. "There are others who would stand by you, including your mother, Garthayn. We would head for the Great Treasure Hoard and stop halfway, then I alone would go on further and rally those who despise Glaider, and we would beset the Black Terror before he knew we were there. There are strong numbers of us who want nothing more than to root out and bring to an end this foe's reign."

This, no doubt, sounded appealing to Weltheron. He knew he could no longer run from the coming storm, but he also didn't want to leave his friends, those like Starmane, Uriel, and Casmin. But already enough blood had been spilled on his account, and he wanted no more of it.

"Very well," he said. "It is half a day's flight back to the Great Treasure Hoard. We must leave now before those of Maladron know you are here."

And with that, both father and son departed west to reunite with those of their kind and to deal with Glaider themselves.

The sun had risen out of the east, its light spilling over Maladron's fields, which were lightly covered in snow. Crestlin had awakened; it was the ninth hour, and one of the Ëmerels was also awake. Inside the citadel, there were no extending rooms but one large one. All its floors, walls, and ceiling were rough-cut pine wood. Intersecting wooden beams upheld the interior of its roof, and hanging from the walls were arrayed banners representing each house of the realm. On the floor in front of the hall's gates, spread out before the threshold, was a thick fleece of bear skin. Off to the left, there was a stone fireplace with a large hewn mantel made of oak, and in the middle of the hall, was a long wooden table. This extended straight back with the throne at the head. Of course, this seat of honor was the king's during every meal, and on either side of him were thrones as well. These belonged to his wife and son—or they used to, since they were dead now and had left these chairs vacant.

It didn't take long before Helmondëm and Andróf arrived that day. The lord of the Fairlands brought with him another five thousand of his kin and even some of his maidens, who came with all sorts of food and supplies, including rations for Crestlin's people. Most were bushels of sweet corn and grains of wheat, which had been freshly harvested. All these provisions they transported in wagons and carts, pulled by large antelope, tamed beasts that inhabited the Fairlands.

The worlaug chieftain also came bearing gifts of his own. He came with three thousand of his giants and brought with him five skewered wild boar, which two rhinoceros beasts had packed on their backs, all the way from Tybran. The gates of the fortress were pulled open, and both foreign lords entered. Helmondëm had ridden all the way to Maladron on Crestlin's steed, returning him to his master's care.

Both the fairwing and worlaug armies remained outside the walls. The lords' arrival was announced with a horn blown by watchmen atop the parapets. The horn alerted Crestlin, who, once hearing it, arose and made for the hall's gates. The villagers appreciated and accepted such gifts, and they would soon indulge in all these. Crestlin, clad in grey leather garments, went out to greet Helmondëm and Andróf. One of the Ëmerels followed closely behind him.

"Welcome, friends," said Crestlin. "I see you have both come bearing gifts. My people and I thank you. I see too that you have brought with you my steed, which I was forced to leave behind Helmondëm."

"Stay your gratitude, O King," replied Helmondëm, stepping down from the saddle. "It did take us longer than it would have to arrive here, but I quite enjoyed it since I have never ridden a beast such as this before. We owe you a great debt, for it was your people's blood that was spilled most in this war, including those of your family. Accept from us these meager tokens of friendship and loyalty."

"Hurorah, the winged master speaks for the both of us," added Andróf.

Crestlin was gladdened to see unity between both of his allies.

Then the king said, "Come then, Helmondëm and Andróf. Come into my hall and warm yourselves by the fire, for the day is cold, and you both must be weary and tired from your journey."

"We shall," said Helmondëm. And turning toward the other, who was the Ëmerel, he said to him, "But first, might I ask you, magician, where is your dragon? I thought he stayed here as well, or have you sent him on an errand elsewhere?"

At hearing this, Casmin was beset in mind. "He is not on guard outside the fortress?" asked the Enchanter.

"Nay, we did not see him there. You do not know where he has gone, magician?"

"No, I do not." Then suddenly resounding thunder was heard amid the skies, but it was too cold for a storm. The Weather Shaper looked troubled. "Maybe he has gone. Maybe he has gone to challenge him," he uttered to himself in a hushed tone.

"What are you saying, magician? Challenge whom?" asked Crestlin.

"Maybe he has gone to challenge Glaider by himself. Where is the other Ëmerel, my comrade, Jack?"

"His bed of straw inside was empty. I assumed you knew," remarked Crestlin.

"How about the stables? Is his reindeer there?" Then the rest of them went to the stables nearby, and upon entering them, they didn't find Jack's reindeer, only the pegasus, Starmane, who stood inside one of the many stalls lining the walls.

Casmin asked him. "Where is Jack's reindeer?"

The pegasus remarked, "The Frost Master took him out early this morning and told me he wanted to let him graze. Why, is he gone?"

"Yes, and I think I know where. I think he has gone after Winter Destiny, who is also missing."

"Good gracious me!" said Starmane.

"We must leave at once!" said Casmin, leading his beast out of his enclosed booth.

"My army is already assembled outside," said Helmondëm. "You and the worlaugs must stay here, Crestlin, for we must be swift in order to find and protect our greatest ally. Casmin and I will go this time."

"No, I must come!" said Crestlin. "I do not fear the wrath of dragons. Our plan was to strike with all our forces!"

"Lord Helmondëm is right, Crestlin. If it comes to it, this will be a battle of the skies, and we must have stealth as well as speed. Stay here and guard your people. You are the only hope if we do not return."

The lord of men had no choice but to submit to what his friends told him. Mounting his pegasus, Casmin rode out of the stables; and once under the misty overcast of cloud, he lifted off the ground, holding on tightly to the mane of his pegasus. Every one of the elves followed after Helmondëm as he also soared high. All adhered to his summoning, and once nearly all of them were a distance off, another odd fairwing took flight. This one, though, wasn't a warrior but one of the maidens who had come with Helmondëm. It was Saylif, and before she departed, she had stared back at Crestlin, and their eyes met. This was Crestlin's first encounter with the daughter of Helmondëm, only he didn't know it, and he was mysteriously taken by her beauty at first glance.

As she climbed higher, the lord of Hilgard with a smile wondered who this beautiful winged elf was, who spawned such an attraction in him. There and then, he made it a point to find out her name when she returned. He also wondered why she, the only maiden, followed Helmondëm and his armed host.

It was around noon when Weltheron and Sëiron neared the Slithering River, which flowed twenty-eight leagues from the Claw. On either side of the Slithering River, which too fed off the coast of Ëmerel-DUL, were the Fells of Hemrod, hills and valleys covering the land for miles and miles. Both dragons caught their breath, resting amid a group of low-bearing hills, inhabited with nothing except ferns; and from here, they found a clear view of the mountains yonder. From these highlands, one could see the Great Mountain towering high above them.

"This is the halfway point," mentioned Sëiron. "Now I must go on alone. I will return with other Raiders. Glaider will think other swarms of dragons have gone out in search of you, my son, and hopefully they will turn a blind eye."

"I will wait here for you," replied Weltheron. "Be careful. Glaider is not like other dragons and is by far more cunning and sly."

Having said this, Weltheron and Sëiron rested their heads against each other as all dragons did as a sign of farewell. Then Sëiron was off, riding the wind as he passed over hills at a tremendous speed. Once he approached a landscape of woods, other dragons surprised him from behind. These beasts hid themselves from below and came at Sëiron, swarming around him like bats. They clawed at him with their talons and bit at the old and helpless Raider, who tried with all his strength to fend them off, but his efforts were no match against them all. There were seven of these Raiders, and they didn't stay their hand, not even for one of their own. Weltheron had seen everything and watched this horrific sight take place before his eyes.

He wanted to rush to his father's aid but was gripped by fear and also didn't want to give himself away. After these merciless Raiders mauled him, Sëiron could take no more and fell out of the sky like a falling star, twirling over and over until he met the surface with a hard impact.

Now Winter Destiny was triggered. He didn't care whether he revealed himself, and without hesitation, he charged this swarm of dragons, who had attacked his father. Without any warning, a great force suddenly knocked him aside, causing him to stumble and stagger in flight. He had fallen a great distance of a hundred feet until finally catching the wind under him. It wasn't until a darkness came over Weltheron that he realized who had surprised him.

It was Glaider. And gazing up at his opponent, Weltheron saw that the Black Terror bore a harsh look Weltheron had never forgotten from when he first encountered the monster. Winter Destiny, despite the fear he bore inside, soared back up to meet this foe, seeking to avenge his father.

Glaider pursued the attack, and once both dragons came face-to-face, they unleashed storms of fire and frost on each other. After failing to prevail in this kind of combat, Glaider then coiled his long tail around and clutched Weltheron by the throat with it, choking the smaller dragon while suspending him in midair. Trying to free himself from his opponent's grip, Weltheron could hardly breathe. He somehow managed to let loose a blast of frost, blinding Glaider and causing him to let go. Roaring and thrashing about, Glaider tried to rid himself of the ice masking his face.

Now it was Weltheron's turn to show his strength, and while his opponent was busy trying to shake free of the blinding ice, Weltheron tried waking the same power he had unleashed during the battle of Maladron, but nothing happened. Either he couldn't think straight or fear had overcome him. There was soon no time as Glaider scraped away the last of the sleet from his face, so Weltheron was forced to wield his frost again. This time he sent a bigger blast that covered not only Glaider's head but also his entire body, causing all of it to stiffen up. Weltheron watched his foe plummet, now held captive by a sheath of ice.

As the pale dragon looked on, he mysteriously noticed something strange. The ice holding Glaider captive suddenly began to crack. This change alarmed Weltheron, who quickly decided to pursue his enemy as he sought to reinforce the shield of ice, but it was by then too late. The Black Terror had broken free and, once mobile again, tussled with Winter Destiny the rest of the way down. They both crashed into a low-bearing valley, both revealing their sharp talons and brawling and striking each other. The frost-breather leapt at the fire-breather, trying to loosen his scale, but it was no use, since his was thicker and bore a strong magic, one no amount of force could seem to penetrate.

The Black Terror, triggering his magic helm by some mysterious force, lifted Winter Destiny off the ground. Lowering his horns, he pulled the frost-breather toward him so rapidly that, upon impact, Weltheron was pierced through the chest. His scale loosened, and the breath was driven out of him. Then Glaider threw Weltheron aside as if he were nothing, and afterward he slowly strode up behind him to finish him off. Weltheron tried to get back up, but he was too badly hurt. From his trunk ran blood like a flowing river.

Glaider now stood over Weltheron and scoffed, saying, "This is it? This is Winter Destiny, who I heard laid waste my scheme to turn others below the mountains against each another, the one who helped defeat my vast army, destroyed those of my own making, and wielded the Star Fire? You are a disgrace, as I once said before, but now you won't have to carry that burden. I will relieve you of it once I kill you."

Then, raising one of his sharpened talons, he was about to drive it into his opponent's neck. But instantly there was a voice from behind him.

"Wait!" said the voice, which sounded familiar only to Weltheron.

Glaider, quickly turning about, spied a young man, who sat astride a beast. It was Jack Winter. Upon his reindeer, he boldly approached the terrifying dragon, with arms outstretched as if surrendering. And that's just what Jack was doing.

"Wait," he said again. "You remember me, don't you, Glaider, whom all call the Black Terror? I know who you are. Rather, that's who you once were."

Gazing down at the Frost Master, Glaider slightly turned his head as if in thought. Then as if recalling, he motioned his crown up and down. "Yesssss," he remarked in a slithering voice as his countenance changed. "You are one of them, the Ëmerels ... that wretched order of magicians who keep a watchful eye over everything that lives and moves. You are one of those who are sworn to bring peace and prosperity to the land. You defy me with your presence here, keeper of Semper!"

"Come now, you were once a keeper yourself, Ganther," replied Jack. "Ganther? No, no, no, there is no Ganther! That fool bargained his soul away long ago when he saw a destiny to rule over this land rather than to be ruled. What are you trying to do to us, magician? You will die, and this world will burn. We've had a vision. The age of dragons has come at last, and we shall rule over this kingdom as one.

"Has Ganther the Concealer, the once-wise magician, forgotten the danger of altering destinies, which Semper himself forbade our order from doing?"

"Speak for yourself, fool, for this white dragon I have just beaten here, this defect that lies slain, couldn't have risen from any such spawn of dragon without the help of magic. He is anything but a dragon, as he does not breathe fire but frost. Sound familiar, Frost Master?"

This strong remark by Glaider weighed heavily on Jack's integrity, and guilt crept over him. He had broken his order's gravest rule, but now he would account for his mistake. He said to Glaider, "The white dragon, which you are about to kill—spare his life. And in exchange, I will give you something you cannot refuse, something that will ensure the destiny you have chosen."

Glaider was intrigued and asked the Ëmerel, "And what is it that you offer, fool?"

"My life. I will trade my life for his. If you kill the frost-breather, what's to prevent me from making others like him—if you spare him, that is. Otherwise you know what I'm capable of, Black Terror. The other Ëmerel and I won't rest until you are purged from this land if you break our bargain!" said Jack bluntly.

This offer was appealing to Glaider, who after hearing the magician's terms thought for a good moment and, once agreeing to this, scoffed, "You have a bargain, fool. I will spare the frost-breather, but you—I will make your death a grueling one, one that will make you wish you had never made such a deal in the first place. Your dragon is dying anyways, so why not?"

Jack Winter, unaware that he was surrounded, was abruptly yanked from his reindeer by one of the other dragons. They not only seized him but feasted on his reindeer. Wrenching the groaning animal in half, they devoured it quickly. They then carried Jack alive back to the Great Treasure Hoard.

Before returning with the rest of the Raiders, Glaider bent low to the ground and whispered in Weltheron's ear, "You have lost. Nothing can stop me now. You think the one you challenged was Glaider. Nay, for I am Mendax, and I feed Glaider his powers and use his body as a host. I have driven Semper far from this land so he can no longer feed you the thing I fear most, the Star Fire, so do me a favor, white dragon, and die."

After he said this, the Black Terror, spreading his vast wings, took flight, leaving Winter Destiny behind to lick his wounds.

11

KNOW YOUR DESTINY

"WE MUST HURRY," said Casmin to his steed, Starmane.

"I'm going as fast as I can, Master. These wind currents are making it difficult to glide since they are against me."

Then Casmin, working his magic, shifted the winds so his winged friend wasn't exerting himself and could fly with the wind at his back. They were near the fells lying on either side of the Slithering River and approaching a low-bearing valley.

"What is that down there amid the boulders?" said Casmin to his steed. "It looks like two slain dragons, and one of them is white. It is Weltheron! Hurry, we must descend now!"

As steadily as he could, Starmane hovered to the ground. Stepping down from the pegasus, Casmin strode over to the wounded dragon. He knelt at the beast's side and gradually put a hand on the frost-breather's head.

"Is he alive?" asked Starmane.

"He's lost a great deal of blood," remarked Casmin, noticing a puddle of red that stained the blades of grass. Just then, landing amid them, were Helmondëm and Uriel with their army.

Weltheron's breathing was labored, as if his heart were beginning to fail him. His eyes were slightly shut, and his nostrils bobbed up and down, releasing small counts of ether. He couldn't move or speak, and with every breath he took, he sounded as though he were groaning, like the wisps of wind whistling through the air.

"What has happened here?" asked Helmondëm, who looked troubled.

"This is the wrath of Glaider. His power seems to have grown by the look of things, but how much, I didn't realize until now," he said with a devastating look. "This creature is close to death, and I do not possess the power to heal it. If only Jack were here, he might be able to help."

The Enchanter then stood upright. Those who stood by could only watch this rare dragon slowly fade before their eyes. But what they all didn't expect was someone else. All the warriors standing behind their lord and prince gradually parted like a veil being drawn, and out from them stepped Saylif, her eyes fixed on the dragon.

Helmondëm, turning around and once realizing she was there, was surprised but too worried. "My daughter! What are you doing here? You were supposed to stay back in Maladron. It is not safe for you here!"

"He's stronger than this. I know he is," said Saylif, gazing into Helmondëm's eyes. Hers were drenched in tears. "You must believe me, Father. Last night I had a dream. It felt so real. I dreamed I saw this dragon. He was hurt bad and could not stand, but what I saw in him most was a fear, a fear that crippled the stronger magic in him. He has only to let go of the fear that holds him captive if he is to rise again. Then Saylif, who bore pity in her heart for the dragon, went over to Weltheron and knelt at his side. She wept bitterly and, closing her eyes, rested one of her hands on the dragon's neck and calmly started to speak; then a song was born from what she knew to be true in her heart.

Awake, you sleeper. Arise, frost-breather,
And know your destiny.

Awake, you endeavor. Let your heart
Be not sever and know your destiny.

Arise from your slumber. Your days are not numbered.
You've just stumbled along the way.

Arise, my defender, you white ascender.
The day is almost at an end.
You cannot leave us. You must save us … again.
You're more than you know,
Not a beast but a friend.

So awake, you sleeper. Arise, frost-breather.
Ere the sun sets, I must detest.
Awake, awake,
And know your destiny.

As Saylif's song ended, the wind shifted again, and the pool of blood that soaked the ground suddenly rushed back into the dragon, and with it, life. The two deep wounds from Glaider that Weltheron bore in his chest grew over again, flesh and scale. The dragon, as if coming out of a deep sleep, slowly opened his eyes and gazing about. He saw tilted over him the fairwing Saylif.

"It is you, fair one," said Weltheron to her.

Saylif, with tears now subsided, with a look of joy answered, "I knew there was more magic to you than this." Stepping back, she let the dragon up.

Once Weltheron was on his feet, Casmin asked, "How is it that Glaider did not kill you and was gone before we arrived?"

"The Frost Master," replied Weltheron. "I couldn't see him, but I heard his voice after I suffered the fatal blow. He gave his life in exchange for mine and was taken back to the Great Treasure Hoard. He followed me and my father all the way here, and this I was unaware of until Mendax attacked me!"

"Mendax! Who is Mendax?" retorted Casmin, a look of bewilderment on his face.

"He is the one who controls Glaider. We were, all of us, deceived into thinking Glaider was the one in charge," remarked Weltheron. "This one who calls himself Mendax told me he drove Semper from this land, which is why I was unable to wield the Star Fire against him and was nearly killed."

"This is, above all, disturbing!" said Casmin. "For a foe like this to cause Semper to flee means only one thing. He must be a thieving deity, one who invades worlds by corrupting the weak in mind and uses them to build up his power. We must find a way to stop this Mendax before he becomes too strong."

"Indeed," remarked Weltheron. "I have never felt such fear before as I felt when I battled this foe, who possessed Glaider." Then Winter Destiny remembered something or someone he had forgotten about. "My father!" he said in distress. "He lies further in the overgrowth yonder, either hurt bad or worse ... dead!"

Immediately the frost-breather hurried over to where Sëiron lay. The rest of them followed him. Once reaching the place, the white dragon strode up to the fallen dragon's side. Sëiron's eyes were half open, but he didn't breathe and was riddled from top to bottom with blood. Much of his scale had been loosened, which accounted for his deep wounds. The frost-breather nudged his father's head as if trying to wake him up, but it was no use. Sëiron the Brown was dead and had died by the wrath of his own kind.

Tears began to well up in Weltheron's eyes. Now he began to groan for real and out of sadness. "Aroah, aroah, aroah," groaned the dragon. The rest of them stood nearby and were also overcome with grief.

Weltheron then turned, facing west where the Great Treasure Hoard lay. For once, he wasn't even a little afraid of Glaider, and turning back to his friends, he said to them, "I must finish this task alone, for it is my destiny. My kind will not show mercy to you all. You will only be giving them a reason to go to war. You must protect your own homes. If I cannot put this evil in its place, no one will. You must trust me." After saying this, he departed. The rest of his friends knew the dragon was right and could only look on as Winter Destiny went to confront his greatest adversary again.

This foe, meanwhile, had the Frost Master brought to the top of the Great Mountain peak. From this high up, there was nothing except a vast drop off, eighteen thousand feet straight down. There was a cloud line that day, which hid everything for leagues. At the summit of the Great Mountain was a flat surface; it was small and extended only several feet in either direction. Jack was held captive up here and, gazing over the edge and peering miles below, beheld the only thing visible to him, and that was the sight of hundreds of dragons. All of them were assembled in a stone valley.

"Like the view?" came a voice suddenly from behind Jack.

Of course, it was Glaider, and while the Frost Master wasn't looking, this beast snuck up behind him. The foe stood behind the Ëmerel, a large dark figure towering over him.

"When there are no clouds, one can see farther than Maladron, but I, on the other hand—I am more, as my vision is stronger than any and can pierce through most anything, including a person's mind. A pity so many don't share in the same vision I do," he teased.

"But you, Frost Master, for some mysterious reason, I cannot read your mind. Yours is like a shield that keeps me out. I seek to know why. Do you have a vision? Everyone does, but most choose not to act on them. You look like someone who has depthththth," he slithered. "We need people like you with knowledge enough to make for themselves their own vision. Don't you agree, Frost Master?"

"And who is *we*, Glaider?" asked Jack. "Whose real vision are you and I to play a part in?"

"My, you are a smart one. You see, you *do* have vision as I said. We serve the one called Mendax. He is neither flesh nor bone and is a spirit that invades worlds. It was only through ones like Ganther that he came to be in Ëmerel-DUL. Just think. If we ruled this land, the three of us, you wouldn't have to hide away like an outcast. You would rule half this kingdom and not just run a tavern and be paid with measly gold and silver coin. You would sit on an ice-hewn throne, be given a crystal palace to live in, and below the mountains, it would always be winter. I would also give you your own servants. All you have to do is kneel before me and utter the Changing of Destiny, and I would free you of your allegiance to Semper," said Glaider, resting one of his talons on Jack's shoulder.

Thinking for a moment, Jack pondered everything the Black Terror had told him; then, quickly coming to a decision, he remarked, "That all sounds quite appealing, and I do like the idea of it always being winter, but I am quite fond of my looks as well." At hearing this kind of response, Glaider was confused. He didn't know what the Frost Master was talking about.

"Yes, what I mean is," continued Jack, striding to another part of the summit, "I just can't get over the fact of being as big and ugly as you, Glaider. What, did Mendax forget to mention the makeover as you uttered the Changing of Destiny? Besides, not once did I hear that Ganther was a pretty good fellow. All I've heard is fool this and fool that. Don't get me wrong, fire-breather. I like my reputation. I'm just someone who's sold on honesty, and right now, I don't even get the feeling I'm talking to Ganther."

"Treachery, treachery, fool. You have spoken your last breath! I will show you who looks ugly after I'm finished with you," he bellowed and, once unfurling his vast wings, lifted off the peak. A few minutes later, a swarm of Raiders surrounded Jack yet again. This time there were twenty of them, all suspended in the air. Together, they vomited several fire storms down on Jack, who crossed his arms and tried to resist their overwhelming scorch of heat with his magic.

12

THE RENAISSANCE OF DESTINY

Below the Great Treasure Hoard loomed the monster, Glaider. Indeed, he was by now fully turned as the spirit of Mendax possessed his entire being. Resting on a stone perch, the Black Terror addressed all the Raiders yet again, and this time he meant business. "Now has come the time to beset this land. It is not a request, for I order it, as I am your lord! The age of dragons has come at last. We will rule this kingdom and cleanse it of all beings with our fire!" After he said this, among the mass of dragons echoed resounding multitudes of them snarling and stroking their wings. Some multitudes, however, didn't display such fervent reaction to their lord's verdict. These were the ones who didn't respect Glaider, yet they followed his lead and didn't dare to question his bidding.

"The lone defiler, the one they call Winter Destiny below the mountains, is no more, for his wrath came to an end this very day. I killed him and left his carcass for the vultures to feed on. This frost-breather was powerless not only against me but against the one called Mendax, whom I serve. This Mendax that I speak of made me who I am, for I was not always a dragon same as you. I was once a magician, a sorcerer who was beheld to a master who treated me and the rest of my order (three of us there were) like outcasts," admitted Glaider. "But now that has changed, for my new master has freed me from my exile and has bestowed on me greater power. It is his voice you hear when I speak since we are one and the same."

After hearing this, all the Raiders were brought to distress and murmured among themselves. Most were paralyzed with fear, save Garthayn the Grey, the only one who had taken heart and decided to stir up mutiny against Glaider. It was time to stand up to the Black Terror, who had oppressed them long enough (she as well had nothing else to lose since she guessed her son and possibly her mate were now dead).

Restless, Garthayn mounted a stone perch, same as Glaider, and began to speak aloud. "Raiders, do not give in to the wishes of this nomad, this ruthless monster possessed by a demon. He has already renounced his claim as a dragon, and now he commands you to serve him. I say he has no place here and should be driven out. For too long have we endured Glaider the Black. It is time we stand together!" After she said this, there was again heard a number of dragons, but this time most were in favor of Garthayn.

Glaider, spying the Raider who provoked mutiny against him, was brought to anger and sought to kill this other one who defied him. Alighting on the boulder he rested on, he attacked Garthayn. All the other Raiders, seeing their lord go into a fury and charge the female, scattered. Because of this, Garthayn was the only one left to face Glaider, and she alone was no match against him. It was already too late to escape since Glaider was upon her, but out of nowhere appeared Weltheron.

The male dragon surged full speed at Glaider, knocking him aside. Like thunder, Glaider hit the ground, tumbling over and over until his body met the firm structure of a boulder. Minutes after the collision, Glaider rose from his hard fall. "Arrth, arrth," he groaned. "Who dares to come between me and this traitorous Raider!"

"Consider this payback for what you did to me before," said Weltheron, who now stood in front of his mother. The Black Terror, still shaken and at the same time baffled, answered, "You are alive? How can this be? You were on the brink of death, and no one could have healed you, not even Semper, for when he saw the magnitude of my power, his spirit fled this land, leaving it for the taking."

"You think I do not hear the one who altered me speak to my thoughts as well, you who call yourself Glaider?" replied Weltheron. "When you left me for dead, the Frost Master, whom you ceased, healed me. I had only to let go of my fear that held me captive inside. This Frost Master is not who you think he is, enslaver of Glaider. You may have deceived all of us, but what you do not realize is that you yourself have been deceived in thinking Semper has fled ... Indeed he is here. The one called Frost Master is Semper and has been here all along."

"No, it cannot be!" roared Glaider. "Mendax drove his spirit away. He has fled! Now I will finish what I failed to do before, and that is killing you, Winter Destiny. Then I will attend to Semper, and once I am finished with both of you, I will turn this entire kingdom into a wasteland, and all will burn," vowed Glaider and attacked Weltheron.

The two of them resumed where they had left off. Some of the Raiders who were loyal to Glaider joined in the brawling, not heeding the rules of a fair fight. When this happened, Garthayn too joined in but fought to defend her son, who was already being overpowered, and there came to be a great division among all the Raiders. Throughout the valley were heard roars and cries of beasts.

Amid all this, above the cloud line looming over the valley, midpoint of the Great Treasure Hoard, Casmin flew upon his pegasus. He had used this haze to his advantage to conceal his rescuing Jack from his place of isolation atop the Great Mountain. Before mutiny had occurred below the Great Mountain, the Frost Master had endured hours of torture by fire and started to slowly dissolve of his humanlike form. It wasn't until his torturers left him to himself and retreated back down to the surface that he realized there was a battle raging below. Meanwhile, in their absence, Casmin made his move and urged Starmane up there, and once landing amid the mountaintop, Starmane rushed to his friend's side.

A slight cold breeze whistled by up there. Jack knelt on two legs wearily, his head bent, his eyes closed, and his arms sprawled outward. His body was riddled with burns, and he was naked since all his clothes had shriveled to nothing from the intense heat. Some of the marks he was covered in glistened like glazed frost and were signs that Jack's power was slowly deserting him.

"Frost, Frost, are you all right?" cried Casmin. The Enchanter, kneeling at his friend's side, held him in his arms.

Jack, hearing his friend's voice, gradually opened his eyes and slowly began to speak. His voice sounded raspy since his throat was very dry.

"You look better than I do right now," replied Jack. "You're a sight for sore eyes, Enchanter."

"Come, we must get you back down the mountain and back to your home in the Freezing Mountains, where your power can heal!" remarked Casmin.

"No, I'm already passing and am not long for this world. This was the plan all along, Enchanter, even before you came to visit me at Snowflake. Even before I uttered the Changing of Destiny, I saw what it would cost me and afterward thought surely I would not have to pay the price if my plan failed. But once you revealed to me at Durnhun that hope did not disappoint, for the first time I had experienced fear, a thing I have never felt before. Tell me," asked Jack, "has Winter Destiny awakened from his sleep of dread?"

At hearing this, Casmin was baffled as to how Jack knew this and answered, "Yes, he has awakened, but how do you know this, old friend?"

"Forgive me, Enchanter, for I am not who you think I am."

Casmin, who misunderstood what Jack meant again, replied, "What are you talking about, Frost? You are my friend, and you did what you thought was right."

"You are indeed a good fellow," responded the Frost Master. "I too consider you a friend and will always be there to guide you.

Semper has never left us and is the one speaking to you at this moment."

When Casmin heard this, he was distraught and, because of how taken back he was, couldn't find the words to say. Then Jack, who now revealed himself to be Semper disguised as one of the Ëmerels, finished the rest of what he wanted to say to Casmin. "It is time to return to my spirit and bring to a completion what I have started." Again he spoke the Changing of Destiny, the Unthinkable Spell that was never to be uttered, but this time he changed its contents.

As he who utters this spell, if it be not in malice,
They dare to foretell.

If it be for the greater good
As it should,
Then as assuredly as they foretold,
So will the one whose destiny is altered will unfold.

Once having said this, the rest of the embodied Semper melted and sank into the surface, vanishing into its sand. The Enchanter, still distraught, wondered why Semper himself, the one who had bidden them never to recite such a powerful spell, had uttered it himself. It wasn't until Casmin and Starmane felt a growing vibration beneath their feet, which soon caused the entire mountain to shake uncontrollably, that Casmin mounted his pegasus and abandoned that place.

The Enchanter wasn't sure whether the mountain was going to erupt like a volcano. As they flew from there in a hurry, a sudden burst of wind met them from behind, nearly causing them to fall out of the sky. This shockwave came forth from the Great Mountain, and once reaching the valley, it did something to all the Raiders who fought from beneath.

The ruthless Glaider pinned Weltheron down on his back when he realized what had happened. The white dragon, who now bore scars across his face, saw his rival gazing above him in disbelief. He turned round to see what it was he was staring at. Nearly every dragon was turned white, and others had turned to stone. Those that had been turned to stone were the ones that followed Glaider, and the ones that were white were those that had fought against him. Semper himself had altered all of them, and they were now frost-breathers like Weltheron.

Now the helm on Glaider's head became visible, and Weltheron saw it, knowing something was happening. Suddenly he heard a familiar voice in his head speak to him like it had done in the past; it was Semper, and he spoke to the pale dragon. *Now is the time to finish Glaider off. His helm has revealed itself, which means his master, Mendax, has fled.*

After he heard this, the magic inside Winter Destiny was aroused again, but this time Weltheron didn't use the Star Fire. From his own helm shone a beam of light, like a laser that, once aligning itself with Glaider's helm, instantly began to burn away at the other helm, causing it to slowly wear off. For several minutes there was the war of the minds. With all the strength he had left, Glaider tried to resist Weltheron's helm, but he couldn't and soon felt an unbearable sting, one that caused him to cry out in torment. The Black Terror was little by little being obliterated. It wasn't until his scale-like form became reduced to ashes and crumbled to the ground that a dark figure eventually stood in its place.

This was Ganther, and he looked hideous to gaze on since his face and body over time had fallen victim to decay. The garments he wore were nothing except rags; all were covered in black soot. His powerful spell had been lifted, and everything about him looked spent, including his power, which he didn't possess anymore. In a rasping voice, Ganther uttered only one word. "How?" And he fell on his face and died.

After this there came a whining sound from above. Upon his pegasus, Casmin landed amid Weltheron and the other dragons. Getting to his feet again, Winter Destiny greeted the Ëmerel, who, once landed, asked the dragon, "What has happened here?" Casmin dismounted his steed and looked around in confusion.

"The Black Terror is no more, and Mendax has fled," remarked Weltheron. "And thanks to the Frost Master—or should I say Semper?"

The Enchanter, gazing at the dragon, answered, "You knew?"

"It was after I met you, magician, that I started hearing his voice in my head but only if I desired to, since I wasn't forced against my will, unlike Glaider, whom Mendax used and held captive inside."

Before Casmin could respond, multitudes of white dragons gradually approached them. Among these albinos was Garthayn, no longer Garthayn the Grey since her scale was now the hue of white, and so were the rest of the other dragons. Weltheron, recognizing her, strode up to his mother, and they both rested their heads against each other but this time in harmony. Once they had done this, Garthayn spoke to her son. "You came back to us, Weltheron, and helped save us from Glaider. I feel ... I feel different inside as I have never felt before. What is this that I feel?"

"I know that feeling. It is freedom, Garthayn," replied Weltheron. "It will only continue to grow, and you will desire nothing. Not even the riches of this world will mean anything to you anymore, not even the great amount of wealth that lies within the Great Treasure Hoard. Above everything, you will grow to desire peace such as I have."

"I wish I had felt this way a long time ago," remarked Garthayn. "If only your father were alive to experience this, he would say the same."

Weltheron, attesting to this, nodded his head up and down

until Casmin interrupted them, saying, "Here lies Ganther the Concealer, and he fooled all of us, including me. But his death is not the end of things to come, for it was Mendax who deceived Ganther and is how such evil entered Ëmerel-DUL. I do not know where his spirit is now, but my guess is, it is not far away, and there are still at large many other tribes of dragons. We must find out what else lies beyond the land that is evil and bring its malice to an end once and for all. Now you, Winter Destiny, are the new lord of this tribe of frost-breathers. I wonder, what shall you call yourselves now if not Raiders anymore?"

Weltheron, with a look of pride on his face, answered Casmin, "From now on, you can call us Protectors," he said, gazing west as the sun was setting.

THE END

ACKNOWLEDGMENTS

I just want to thank all those people who unknowingly inspired me to write this book. First, I want to thank my sister Mary, who has been hounding me to write this book over again. In the past, I have written three other versions of this story until realizing what chemistry was needed to make this book flow.

I especially want to thank my parents, who have been so supportive and helpful in making this happen. I want to thank my mother, who found a publisher for it, and my father, who sat down with me and gave me insightful editorial feedback on it. I want to thank my brother, Francis, as well, who has been helping me create promo videos for this book and future books to come. It has been a lifelong journey for me in writing this story; it took me seven years just to think of the idea and all the characters and places. The first book is always the hardest, but once you've created characters, it is for sure way easier to write sequels, I must say.

When I started rewriting this book for the fourth and final time, I worked for my uncle Rich, doing interior pre-finish work for homes. I met some great people doing work like that, people who gave me confidence. One of my uncle's workers—Chris was his name—gave me some good advice in thinking about what I want to do in life (that I should stop worrying about others and start worrying about me). This helped me realize that if I'm going to do something at all, I need to do it now and not before it's too late. Working with uplifting and encouraging people like this helped me think of ideas as I worked. Every now and then as I used different colors, whether they were stain or paint, I painted a picture in my head of what the world I was envisioning looked like. It was all unfolding into something I now am glad to say was in me all along, I just needed to push aside life's drama and all those things that hold us back from doing what we want.

CPSIA information can be obtained
at www.ICGtesting.com
Printed in the USA
LVHW090147240919
632082LV00001B/23/P